ANTON CHEKHOV

Anton Chekhov, a Russian writer, playwright and physician, considered to be one of the greatest short story writers in the history of world literature. His career as a dramatist produced all-time classics The Seagull, Uncle Vanya, Three Sisters and Cherry Orchard. His short stories are held in high esteem by writers, critics and audiences of all generations. Chekhov practised as a doctor throughout most of his literary career.'Medicine is my lawful wife, and literature is my mistress', he once said.

ANTON CHEKHOV

ARIADNE
& OTHER STORIES

SHORT STORIES BY ANTON CHEKHOV

NEW EDITION
ANNOTATED

TOP 10 World

TOP 10 RUSSIA

SOVEREIGN

SOVEREIGN

LONDON NEW YORK MELBOURNE TORONTO
MOSCOW CAPE TOWN AUCKLAND

New Edition, World Classics
Short Stories by Anton Chekhov
Top 10 of Russian Classics, World Classics, and Top 10 Classics of All-Time

Published by Sovereign
An imprint of Max Bollinger
27 Old Gloucester St,
London WC1N 3AX

sales@anton-chekhov.com
www.anton-chekhov.com

This Edition
First published in 2012

Author: Anton Chekhov
Editor: Max Bollinger

British Library Cataloguing in Publication Data.
A catalogue record for this book is available from the British Library.
Library of Congress Cataloguing in Publication Data.
A catalogue record for this book has been requested.

ISBN: 9781909175761 (pbk)
ISBN: 9781909175600 (ebk)

Bref: ADN-03

CONTENTS

ARIADNE

On the deck of a steamer sailing from Odessa to Sevastopol, a rather good-looking gentleman, with a little round beard, came up to me to smoke, and said:

"Notice those Germans sitting near the shelter? Whenever Germans or Englishmen get together, they talk about the crops, the price of wool, or their personal affairs. But for some reason or other when we Russians get together we never discuss anything but women and abstract subjects—but especially women."

This gentleman's face was familiar to me already. We had returned from abroad the evening before in the same train, and at Volotchisk when the luggage was being examined by the Customs, I saw him standing with a lady, his travelling companion, before a perfect mountain of trunks and baskets filled with ladies' clothes, and I noticed how embarrassed and downcast he was when he had to pay duty on some piece of silk frippery, and his companion protested and threatened to make a complaint. Afterwards, on the way to Odessa, I saw him carrying little pies and oranges to the ladies' compartment.

It was rather damp; the vessel swayed a little, and the ladies had retired to their cabins.

The gentleman with the little round beard sat down beside me and continued:

"Yes, when Russians come together they discuss nothing but abstract subjects and women. We are so intellectual, so solemn, that we utter nothing but truths and can discuss only questions of a lofty order. The Russian actor does not know how to be funny; he acts with profundity even in a farce. We're just the same: when we have got to talk of trifles we treat them only from an exalted point of view. It comes from a lack of boldness, sincerity, and simplicity. We talk so often about women, I fancy, because we are dissatisfied. We take too ideal a view of women, and make demands out of all proportion with what reality can give us; we get something utterly different from what we want, and the result is dissatisfaction, shattered hopes, and inward suffering, and if any one is suffering, he's bound to talk of it. It does not bore you to go on with this conversation?

"No, not in the least."

"In that case, allow me to introduce myself," said my companion, rising from his seat a little:

"Ivan Ilyitch Shamohin, a Moscow landowner of a sort. . . . You I know very well."

He sat down and went on, looking at me with a genuine and friendly expression:

"A mediocre philosopher, like Max Nordau, would explain these incessant conversations about women as a form of erotic madness, or would put it down to our having been slave-owners and so on; I take quite a different view of it. I repeat, we are dissatisfied because we are idealists. We want the creatures who bear us and our children to be superior to us and to everything in the world. When we are young we adore and poeticize those with whom we are in love: love and happiness with us are synonyms. Among us in Russia marriage without love is despised, sensuality is ridiculed and inspires repulsion, and the greatest success is enjoyed by those tales and novels in which women are beautiful, poetical, and exalted; and if the Russian has been for years in ecstasies over Raphael's Madonna, or is eager for the emancipation of women, I assure you there is no affectation about it. But the trouble is that when we have been married or been intimate with a woman for some two or three years, we begin to feel deceived and disillusioned: we pair off with others, and again—disappointment, again—repulsion, and in the long run we become convinced that women are lying, trivial, fussy, unfair, undeveloped, cruel—in fact, far from being superior, are immeasurably inferior to us men. And in our dissatisfaction and disappointment there is nothing left for us but to grumble and talk about what we've been so cruelly deceived in."

While Shamohin was talking I noticed that the Russian language and our Russian surroundings gave him great pleasure. This was probably because he had been very homesick abroad. Though he praised the Russians and ascribed to them a rare idealism, he did not disparage foreigners, and that I put down to his credit. It could be seen, too, that there was some uneasiness in his soul, that he wanted to talk more of himself than of women, and that I was in for a long story in the nature of a confession. And when we had asked for a bottle of wine and had each of us drunk a glass, this was how he did in fact begin:

"I remember in a novel of Weltmann's some one says, 'So that's the story!' and some one else answers, 'No, that's not the story— that's only the introduction to the story.' In the same way what I've said so far is only the introduction; what I really want to tell you is my own love story. Excuse me, I must ask you again; it won't bore you to listen?"

I told him it would not, and he went on:

The scene of my story is laid in the Moscow province in one of its northern districts. The scenery there, I must tell you, is exquisite. Our homestead is on the high bank of a rapid stream, where the water chatters noisily day and night: imagine a big old garden, neat flower-beds, beehives, a kitchen-garden, and below it a river with leafy willows, which, when there is a heavy dew on them, have a lustreless look as though they had turned grey; and on the other side a meadow, and beyond the meadow on the upland a terrible, dark pine forest. In that forest delicious, reddish agarics grow in endless profusion, and elks still live in its deepest recesses. When I am nailed up in my coffin I believe I shall still dream of those early mornings, you know, when the sun hurts your eyes: or the wonderful spring evenings when the nightingales and the landrails call in the garden and beyond the garden, and sounds of the harmonica float across from the village, while they play the piano indoors and the stream babbles . . . when there is such music, in fact, that one wants at the same time to cry and to sing aloud.

We have not much arable land, but our pasture makes up for it, and with the forest yields about two thousand roubles a year. I am the only son of my father; we are both modest persons, and with my father's pension that sum was amply sufficient for us.

The first three years after finishing at the university I spent in the country, looking after the estate and constantly expecting to be elected on some local assembly; but what was most important, I was violently in love with an extraordinarily beautiful and fascinating girl. She was the sister of our neighbour, Kotlovitch, a ruined landowner who had on his estate pine-apples, marvellous peaches, lightning conductors, a fountain in the courtyard, and at the same time not a farthing in his pocket. He did nothing and knew how to do nothing. He was as flabby as though he had been made of boiled turnip; he used to doctor the peasants by homeopathy and was interested in spiritualism. He was, however, a man of great delicacy and mildness, and by no means a fool, but I have no fondness for these gentlemen who converse with spirits and cure peasant women by magnetism. In the first place, the ideas of people who are not intellectually free are always in a muddle, and it's extremely difficult to talk to them; and, secondly, they usually love no one, and have nothing to do with women, and their mysticism has an unpleasant effect on sensitive people. I did not care for his appearance either. He was tall, stout, white-skinned, with a little head, little shining eyes, and chubby white fingers. He did not shake hands, but kneaded one's hands in his. And he was always apologising. If he asked for anything it was "Excuse me"; if he gave you anything it was "Excuse me" too.

As for his sister, she was a character out of a different opera. I must explain that I had not been acquainted with the Kotlovitches in my childhood and early youth, for my father had been a professor at N., and we had for many years lived away. When I did make their acquaintance the girl was twenty-two, had left school long before, and had spent two or three years in Moscow with a wealthy aunt who brought her out into society. When I was introduced and first had to talk to her, what struck me most of all was her rare and beautiful name—Ariadne. It suited her so wonderfully! She was a brunette, very thin, very slender, supple, elegant, and extremely graceful, with refined and exceedingly noble features. Her eyes were shining, too, but her brother's shone with a cold sweetness, mawkish as sugar-candy, while hers had the glow of youth, proud and beautiful. She conquered me on the first day of our acquaintance, and indeed it was inevitable. My first impression was so overwhelming that to this day I cannot get rid of my illusions; I am still tempted to imagine that nature had some grand, marvellous design when she created that girl.

Ariadne's voice, her walk, her hat, even her footprints on the sandy bank where she used to angle for gudgeon, filled me with delight and a passionate hunger for life. I judged of her spiritual being from her lovely face and lovely figure, and every word, every smile of Ariadne's bewitched me, conquered me and forced me to believe in the loftiness of her soul. She was friendly, ready to talk, gay and simple in her manners. She had a poetic belief in God, made poetic reflections about death, and there was such a wealth of varying shades in her spiritual organisation that even her faults seemed in her to carry with them peculiar, charming qualities. Suppose she wanted a new horse and had no money—what did that matter? Something might be sold or pawned, or if the steward swore that nothing could possibly be sold or pawned, the iron roofs might be torn off the lodges and taken to the factory, or at the very busiest time the farm-horses might be driven to the market and sold there for next to nothing.

These unbridled desires reduced the whole household to despair at times, but she expressed them with such refinement that everything was forgiven her; all things were permitted her as to a goddess or to Cæsar's wife. My love was pathetic and was soon noticed by every one—my father, the neighbours, and the peasants—and they all sympathised with me. When I stood the workmen vodka, they would bow and say: "May the Kotlovitch young lady be your bride, please God!"

And Ariadne herself knew that I loved her. She would often ride over on horseback or drive in the char-à-banc to see us, and would spend whole days with me and my father. She made great friends with the old man, and he even taught her to bicycle, which was his favourite amusement.

I remember helping her to get on the bicycle one evening, and she looked so lovely that I felt as though I were burning my hands when I touched her. I shuddered with rapture, and when the two of them, my old father and she, both looking so handsome and elegant, bicycled side by side along the main road, a black horse ridden by the steward dashed aside on meeting them, and it seemed to me that it dashed aside because it too was overcome by her beauty. My love, my worship, touched Ariadne and softened her; she had a passionate longing to be captivated like me and to respond with the same love. It was so poetical!

But she was incapable of really loving as I did, for she was cold and already somewhat corrupted. There was a demon in her, whispering to her day and night that she was enchanting, adorable; and, having no definite idea for what object she was created, or for what purpose life had been given her, she never pictured herself in the future except as very wealthy and distinguished, she had visions of balls, races, liveries, of sumptuous drawing-rooms, of a salon of her own, and of a perfect swarm of counts, princes, ambassadors, celebrated painters and artists, all of them adoring her and in ecstasies over her beauty and her dresses. . . .

This thirst for personal success, and this continual concentration of the mind in one direction, makes people cold, and Ariadne was cold—to me, to nature, and to music. Meanwhile time was passing, and still there were no ambassadors on the scene. Ariadne went on living with her brother, the spiritualist: things went from bad to worse, so that she had nothing to buy hats and dresses with, and had to resort to all sorts of tricks and dodges to conceal her poverty.

As luck would have it, a certain Prince Maktuev, a wealthy man but an utterly insignificant person, had paid his addresses to her when she was living at her aunt's in Moscow. She had refused him, point-blank. But now she was fretted by the worm of repentance that she had refused him; just as a peasant pouts with repulsion at a mug of kvass with cockroaches in it but yet drinks it, so she frowned disdainfully at the recollection of the prince, and yet she would say to me: "Say what you like, there is something inexplicable, fascinating, in a title. . . ."

She dreamed of a title, of a brilliant position, and at the same time she did not want to let me go. However one may dream of ambassadors one's heart is not a stone, and one has wistful feelings for one's youth. Ariadne tried to fall in love, made a show of being in love, and even swore that she loved me. But I am a highly strung and sensitive man; when I am loved I feel it even at a distance, without vows and assurances; at once I felt as it were a coldness in the air, and when she talked to me of love, it seemed to me as though I were listening to the singing of a metal nightingale. Ariadne was herself aware that she was lacking in something. She was vexed and more than once I saw her cry. Another time—can you imagine it?—all of a sudden she embraced me and kissed me. It happened in the evening on the river-bank, and I saw by her eyes that she did not love me, but was embracing me from curiosity, to test herself and to see what came of it. And I felt dreadful. I took her hands and said to her in despair: "These caresses without love cause me suffering!"

"What a queer fellow you are!" she said with annoyance, and walked away.

Another year or two might have passed, and in all probability I should have married her, and so my story would have ended, but fate was pleased to arrange our romance differently. It happened that a new personage appeared on our horizon. Ariadne's brother had a visit from an old university friend called Mihail Ivanitch Lubkov, a charming man of whom coachmen and footmen used to say: "An entertaining gentleman." He was a man of medium height, lean and bald, with a face like a good-natured bourgeois, not interesting, but pale and presentable, with a stiff, well-kept moustache, with a neck like gooseskin, and a big Adam's apple. He used to wear pince-nez on a wide black ribbon, lisped, and could not pronounce either r or l. He was always in good spirits, everything amused him.

He had made an exceedingly foolish marriage at twenty, and had acquired two houses in Moscow as part of his wife's dowry. He began doing them up and building a bath-house, and was completely ruined. Now his wife and four children lodged in Oriental Buildings in great poverty, and he had to support them—and this amused him. He was thirty-six and his wife was by now forty-two, and that, too, amused him. His mother, a conceited, sulky personage, with aristocratic pretensions, despised his wife and lived apart with a perfect menagerie of cats and dogs, and he had to allow her seventy-five roubles a month also; he was, too, a man of taste, liked lunching at the Slavyansky Bazaar and dining at the Hermitage; he needed a great deal of money, but his uncle only allowed him two thousand roubles a year, which was not enough, and for days together he would run about Moscow with his tongue out, as the saying is, looking for some one to borrow from—and this, too, amused him. He had come to Kotlovitch to find in the lap of nature, as he said, a rest from family life. At dinner, at supper, and on our walks, he talked about his wife, about his mother, about his creditors, about the bailiffs, and laughed at them; he laughed at himself and assured us that, thanks to his talent for borrowing, he had made a great number of agreeable acquaintances. He laughed without ceasing and we laughed too. Moreover, in his company we spent our time differently. I was more inclined to quiet, so to say idyllic pleasures; I liked fishing, evening walks, gathering mushrooms; Lubkov preferred picnics, fireworks, hunting. He used to get up picnics three times a week, and Ariadne, with an earnest and inspired face, used to write a list of oysters, champagne, sweets, and used to send me into Moscow to get them, without inquiring, of course, whether I had money. And at the picnics there were toasts and laughter, and again mirthful descriptions of how old his wife was, what fat lap-dogs his mother had, and what charming people his creditors were.

Lubkov was fond of nature, but he regarded it as something long familiar and at the same time, in reality, infinitely beneath himself and created for his pleasure. He would sometimes stand still before some magnificent landscape and say: "It would be nice to have tea here."

One day, seeing Ariadne walking in the distance with a parasol, he nodded towards her and said:

"She's thin, and that's what I like; I don't like fat women."

This made me wince. I asked him not to speak like that about women before me. He looked at me in surprise and said:

"What is there amiss in my liking thin women and not caring for fat ones?"

I made no answer. Afterwards, being in very good spirits and a trifle elevated, he said:

"I've noticed Ariadne Grigoryevna likes you. I can't understand why you don't go in and win."

His words made me feel uncomfortable, and with some embarrassmentI told him how I looked at love and women.

"I don't know," he sighed; "to my thinking, a woman's a woman and a man's a man. Ariadne Grigoryevna may be poetical and exalted, as you say, but it doesn't follow that she must be superior to the laws of nature. You see for yourself that she has reached the age when she must have a husband or a lover. I respect women as much as you do, but I don't think certain relations exclude poetry. Poetry's one thing and love is another. It's just the same as it is in farming. The beauty of nature is one thing and the income from your forests or fields is quite another."

When Ariadne and I were fishing, Lubkov would lie on the sand close by and make fun of me, or lecture me on the conduct of life.

"I wonder, my dear sir, how you can live without a love affair," he would say. "You are young, handsome, interesting—in fact, you're a man not to be sniffed at, yet you live like a monk. Och! I can't stand these fellows who are old at twenty-eight! I'm nearly ten years older than you are, and yet which of us is the younger? Ariadne Grigoryevna, which?"

"You, of course," Ariadne answered him.

And when he was bored with our silence and the attention with which we stared at our floats he went home, and she said, looking at me angrily:

"You're really not a man, but a mush, God forgive me! A man ought to be able to be carried away by his feelings, he ought to be able to be mad, to make mistakes, to suffer! A woman will forgive you audacity and insolence, but she will never forgive your reasonableness!"

She was angry in earnest, and went on:

"To succeed, a man must be resolute and bold. Lubkov is not so handsome as you are, but he is more interesting. He will always succeed with women because he's not like you; he's a man. . . ."

And there was actually a note of exasperation in her voice.

One day at supper she began saying, not addressing me, that if she were a man she would not stagnate in the country, but would travel, would spend the winter somewhere aboard—in Italy, for instance. Oh, Italy! At this point my father unconsciously poured oil on the flames; he began telling us at length about Italy, how splendid it was there, the exquisite scenery, the museums. Ariadne suddenly conceived a burning desire to go to Italy. She positively brought her fist down on the table and her eyes flashed as she said: "I must go!"

After that came conversations every day about Italy: how splendid it would be in Italy—ah, Italy!—oh, Italy! And when Ariadne looked at me over her shoulder, from her cold and obstinate expression I saw that in her dreams she had already conquered Italy with all its salons, celebrated foreigners and tourists, and there was no holding her back now. I advised her to wait a little, to put off her tour for a year or two, but she frowned disdainfully and said:

"You're as prudent as an old woman!"

Lubkov was in favour of the tour. He said it could be done very cheaply, and he, too, would go to Italy and have a rest there from family life.

I behaved, I confess, as naïvely as a schoolboy.

Not from jealousy, but from a foreboding of something terrible and extraordinary, I tried as far as possible not to leave them alone together, and they made fun of me. For instance, when I went in they would pretend they had just been kissing one another, and so on. But lo and behold, one fine morning, her plump, white-skinned brother, the spiritualist, made his appearance and expressed his desire to speak to me alone.

He was a man without will; in spite of his education and his delicacy he could never resist reading another person's letter, if it lay before him on the table. And now he admitted that he had by chance read a letter of Lubkov's to Ariadne.

"From that letter I learned that she is very shortly going abroad. My dear fellow, I am very much upset! Explain it to me for goodness' sake. I can make nothing of it!"

As he said this he breathed hard, breathing straight in my face and smelling of boiled beef.

"Excuse me for revealing the secret of this letter to you, but you are Ariadne's friend, she respects you. Perhaps you know something of it. She wants to go away, but with whom? Mr. Lubkov is proposing to go with her. Excuse me, but this is very strange of Mr. Lubkov; he is a married man, he has children, and yet he is making a declaration of love; he is writing to Ariadne 'darling.' Excuse me, but it is so strange!"

I turned cold all over; my hands and feet went numb and I felt an ache in my chest, as if a three-cornered stone had been driven into it. Kotlovitch sank helplessly into an easy-chair, and his hands fell limply at his sides.

"What can I do?" I inquired.

"Persuade her. . . . Impress her mind. . . . Just consider, what is Lubkov to her? Is he a match for her? Oh, good God! How awful it is, how awful it is!" he went on, clutching his head. "She has had such splendid offers—Prince Maktuev and . . . and others. The prince adores her, and only last Wednesday week his late grandfather, Ilarion, declared positively that Ariadne would be his wife—positively! His grandfather Ilarion is dead, but he is a wonderfully intelligent person; we call up his spirit every day."

After this conversation I lay awake all night and thought of shooting myself. In the morning I wrote five letters and tore them all up. Then I sobbed in the barn. Then I took a sum of money from my father and set off for the Caucasus without saying good-bye.

Of course, a woman's a woman and a man's a man, but can all that be as simple in our day as it was before the Flood, and can it be that I, a cultivated man endowed with a complex spiritual organisation, ought to explain the intense attraction I feel towards a woman simply by the fact that her bodily formation is different from mine? Oh, how awful that would be! I want to believe that in his struggle with nature the genius of man has struggled with physical love too, as with an enemy, and that, if he has not conquered it, he has at least succeeded in tangling it in a net-work of illusions of brotherhood and love; and for me, at any rate, it is no longer a simple instinct of my animal nature as with a dog or a toad, but is real love, and every embrace is spiritualised by a pure impulse of the heart and respect for the woman. In reality, a disgust for the animal instinct has been trained for ages in hundreds of generations; it is inherited by me in my blood and forms part of my nature, and if I poetize love, is not that as natural and inevitable in our day as my ears' not being able to move and my not being covered with fur? I fancy that's how the majority of civilised people look at it, so that the absence of the moral, poetical element in love is treated in these days as a phenomenon, as a sign of atavism; they say it is a symptom of degeneracy, of many forms of insanity. It is true that, in poetizing love, we assume in those we love qualities that are lacking in them, and that is a source of continual mistakes and continual miseries for us. But to my thinking it is better, even so;

that is, it is better to suffer than to find complacency on the basis of woman being woman and man being man.

In Tiflis I received a letter from my father. He wrote that Ariadne Grigoryevna had on such a day gone abroad, intending to spend the whole winter away. A month later I returned home. It was by now autumn. Every week Ariadne sent my father extremely interesting letters on scented paper, written in an excellent literary style. It is my opinion that every woman can be a writer. Ariadne described in great detail how it had not been easy for her to make it up with her aunt and induce the latter to give her a thousand roubles for the journey, and what a long time she had spent in Moscow trying to find an old lady, a distant relation, in order to persuade her to go with her. Such a profusion of detail suggested fiction, and I realised, of course, that she had no chaperon with her.

Soon afterwards I, too, had a letter from her, also scented and literary. She wrote that she had missed me, missed my beautiful, intelligent, loving eyes. She reproached me affectionately for wasting my youth, for stagnating in the country when I might, like her, be living in paradise under the palms, breathing the fragrance of the orange-trees. And she signed herself "Your forsaken Ariadne." Two days later came another letter in the same style, signed "Your forgotten Ariadne." My mind was confused. I loved her passionately, I dreamed of her every night, and then this "your forsaken," "your forgotten"—what did it mean? What was it for? And then the dreariness of the country, the long evenings, the disquieting thoughts of Lubkov. . . . The uncertainty tortured me, and poisoned my days and nights; it became unendurable. I could not bear it and went abroad.

Ariadne summoned me to Abbazzia. I arrived there on a bright warm day after rain; the rain-drops were still hanging on the trees and glistening on the huge, barrack-like dépendance where Ariadne and Lubkov were living.

They were not at home. I went into the park; wandered about the avenues, then sat down. An Austrian General, with his hands behind him, walked past me, with red stripes on his trousers such as our generals wear. A baby was wheeled by in a perambulator and the wheels squeaked on the damp sand. A decrepit old man with jaundice passed, then a crowd of Englishwomen, a Catholic priest, then the Austrian General again. A military band, only just arrived from Fiume, with glittering brass instruments, sauntered by to the bandstand—they began playing.

Have you ever been at Abbazzia? It's a filthy little Slav town with only one street, which stinks, and in which one can't walk after rain without goloshes. I had read so much and always with such intense feeling about this earthly paradise that when afterwards, holding up my trousers, I cautiously crossed the narrow street, and in my ennui bought some hard pears from an old peasant woman who, recognising me as a Russian, said: "Tcheeteery" for "tchetyry" (four)—"davadtsat" for "dvadtsat" (twenty), and when I wondered in perplexity where to go and what to do here, and when I inevitably met Russians as disappointed as I was, I began to feel vexed and ashamed. There is a calm bay there full of steamers and boats with coloured sails. From there I could see Fiume and the distant islands covered with lilac mist, and it would have been picturesque if the view over the bay had not been hemmed in by the hotels and their dépendances—buildings in an absurd, trivial style of architecture, with which the whole of that green shore has been covered by greedy money grubbers, so that for the most part you see nothing in this little paradise but windows, terraces, and little squares with tables and waiters black coats. There is a park such as you find now in every watering-place abroad. And the dark, motionless, silent foliage of the palms, and the bright yellow sand in the avenue, and the bright green seats, and the glitter of the braying military horns—all this sickened me in ten minutes! And yet one is obliged for some reason to spend ten days, ten weeks, there!

Having been dragged reluctantly from one of these watering-places to another, I have been more and more struck by the inconvenient and niggardly life led by the wealthy and well-fed, the dulness and feebleness of their imagination, the lack of boldness in their tastes and desires. And how much happier are those tourists, old and young, who, not having the money to stay in hotels, live where they can, admire the view of the sea from the tops of the mountains, lying on the green grass, walk instead of riding, see the forests and villages at close quarters, observe the customs of the country, listen to its songs, fall in love with its women. . . .

While I was sitting in the park, it began to get dark, and in the twilight my Ariadne appeared, elegant and dressed like a princess; after her walked Lubkov, wearing a new loose-fitting suit, bought probably in Vienna.

"Why are you cross with me?" he was saying. "What have I done to you?"

Seeing me, she uttered a cry of joy, and probably, if we had not been in the park, would have thrown herself on my neck. She pressed my hands warmly and laughed; and I laughed too and almost cried with emotion. Questions followed, of the village, of my father, whether I had seen her brother, and so on. She insisted on my looking her straight in the face, and asked if I remembered the gudgeon, our little quarrels, the picnics. . . .

"How nice it all was really!" she sighed. "But we're not having a slow time here either. We have a great many acquaintances, my dear, my best of friends! To-morrow I will introduce you to a Russian family here, but please buy yourself another hat." She scrutinised me and frowned. "Abbazzia is not the country," she said; "here one must be comme il faut."

Then we went to the restaurant. Ariadne was laughing and mischievous all the time; she kept calling me "dear," "good," "clever," and seemed as though she could not believe her eyes that I was with her. We sat on till eleven o'clock, and parted very well satisfied both with the supper and with each other.

Next day Ariadne presented me to the Russian family as: "The son of a distinguished professor whose estate is next to ours."

She talked to this family about nothing but estates and crops, and kept appealing to me. She wanted to appear to be a very wealthy landowner, and did, in fact, succeed in doing so. Her manner was superb like that of a real aristocrat, which indeed she was by birth.

"But what a person my aunt is!" she said suddenly, looking at me with a smile. "We had a slight tiff, and she has bolted off to Meran. What do you say to that?"

Afterwards when we were walking in the park I asked her:

"What aunt were you talking of just now? What aunt is that?"

"That was a saving lie," laughed Ariadne. "They must not know I'm without a chaperon."

After a moment's silence she came closer to me and said:

"My dear, my dear, do be friends with Lubkov. He is so unhappy! His wife and mother are simply awful."

She used the formal mode of address in speaking to Lubkov, and when she was going up to bed she said good-night to him exactly as she did to me, and their rooms were on different floors. All this made me hope that it was all nonsense, and that there was no sort of love affair between them, and I felt at ease when I met him. And when one day he asked me for the loan of three hundred roubles, I gave it to him with the greatest pleasure.

Every day we spent in enjoying ourselves and in nothing but enjoying ourselves; we strolled in the park, we ate, we drank. Every day there were conversations with the Russian family. By degrees I got used to the fact that if I went into the park I should be sure to meet the old man with jaundice, the Catholic priest, and the Austrian General, who always carried a pack of little cards, and wherever it was possible sat down and played patience, nervously twitching his shoulders. And the band played the same thing over and over again.

At home in the country I used to feel ashamed to meet the peasants when I was fishing or on a picnic party on a working day; here too I was ashamed at the sight of the footmen, the coachmen, and the workmen who met us. It always seemed to me they were looking at me and thinking: "Why are you doing nothing?" And I was conscious of this feeling of shame every day from morning to night. It was a strange, unpleasant, monotonous time; it was only varied by Lubkov's borrowing from me now a hundred, now fifty guldens, and being suddenly revived by the money as a morphia-maniac is by morphia, beginning to laugh loudly at his wife, at himself, at his creditors.

At last it began to be rainy and cold. We went to Italy, and I telegraphed to my father begging him for mercy's sake to send me eight hundred roubles to Rome. We stayed in Venice, in Bologna, in Florence, and in every town invariably put up at an expensive hotel, where we were charged separately for lights, and for service, and for heating, and for bread at lunch, and for the right of having dinner by ourselves. We ate enormously. In the morning they gave us café complet; at one o'clock lunch: meat, fish, some sort of omelette, cheese, fruits, and wine. At six o'clock dinner of eight courses with long intervals, during which we drank beer and wine. At nine o'clock tea. At midnight Ariadne would declare she was hungry, and ask for ham and boiled eggs. We would eat to keep her company.

In the intervals between meals we used to rush about the museums and exhibitions in continual anxiety for fear we should be late for dinner or lunch. I was bored at the sight of the pictures; I longed to be at home to rest; I was exhausted, looked about for a chair and hypocritically repeated after other people: "How exquisite, what atmosphere!" Like overfed boa constrictors, we noticed only the most glaring objects. The shop windows hypnotised us; we went into ecstasies over imitation brooches and bought a mass of useless trumpery.

The same thing happened in Rome, where it rained and there was a cold wind. After a heavy lunch we went to look at St. Peter's, and thanks to our replete condition and perhaps the bad weather, it made no sort of impression on us, and detecting in each other an indifference to art, we almost quarrelled.

The money came from my father. I went to get it, I remember, in the morning. Lubkov went with me.

"The present cannot be full and happy when one has a past," said he. "I have heavy burdens left on me by the past. However, if only I get the money, it's no great matter, but if not, I'm in a fix. Would you believe it, I have only eight francs left, yet I must send my wife a hundred and my mother another. And we must live here too. Ariadne's like a child; she won't enter into the position, and flings away money like a duchess. Why did she buy a watch yesterday? And, tell me, what object is there in our going on playing at being good children? Why, our hiding our relations from the servants and our friends costs us from ten to fifteen francs a day, as I have to have a separate room. What's the object of it?"

I felt as though a sharp stone had been turned round in my chest. There was no uncertainty now; it was all clear to me. I turned cold all over, and at once made a resolution to give up seeing them, to run away from them, to go home at once. . . .

"To get on terms with a woman is easy enough," Lubkov went on. "You have only to undress her; but afterwards what a bore it is, what a silly business!"

When I counted over the money I received he said:

"If you don't lend me a thousand francs, I am faced with complete ruin. Your money is the only resource left to me."

I gave him the money, and he at once revived and began laughing about his uncle, a queer fish, who could never keep his address secret from his wife. When I reached the hotel I packed and paid my bill. I had still to say good-bye to Ariadne.

I knocked at the door.

"Entrez!"

In her room was the usual morning disorder: tea-things on the table, an unfinished roll, an eggshell; a strong overpowering reek of scent. The bed had not been made, and it was evident that two had slept in it.

Ariadne herself had only just got out of bed and was now with her hair down in a flannel dressing-jacket.

I said good-morning to her, and then sat in silence for a minute while she tried to put her hair tidy, and then I asked her, trembling all over:

"Why . . . why . . . did you send for me here?"

Evidently she guessed what I was thinking; she took me by the hand and said:

"I want you to be here, you are so pure."

I felt ashamed of my emotion, of my trembling. And I was afraid I might begin sobbing, too! I went out without saying another word, and within an hour I was sitting in the train. All the journey, for some reason, I imagined Ariadne with child, and she seemed disgusting to me, and all the women I saw in the trains and at the stations looked to me, for some reason, as if they too were with child, and they too seemed disgusting and pitiable. I was in the position of a greedy, passionate miser who should suddenly discover that all his gold coins were false. The pure, gracious images which my imagination, warmed by love, had cherished for so long, my plans, my hopes, my memories, my ideas of love and of woman—all now were jeering and putting out their tongues at me. "Ariadne," I kept asking with horror, "that young, intellectual, extraordinarily beautiful girl, the daughter of a senator, carrying on an intrigue with such an ordinary, uninteresting vulgarian? But why should she not love Lubkov?" I answered myself. "In what is he inferior to me? Oh, let her love any one she likes, but why lie to me? But why is she bound to be open with me?" And so I went on over and over again till I was stupefied.

It was cold in the train; I was travelling first class, but even so there were three on a side, there were no double windows, the outer door opened straight into the compartment, and I felt as though I were in the stocks, cramped, abandoned, pitiful, and my legs were fearfully numb, and at the same time I kept recalling how fascinating she had been that morning in her dressing-jacket and with her hair down, and I was suddenly overcome by such acute jealousy that I leapt up in anguish, so that my neighbours stared at me in wonder and positive alarm.

At home I found deep snow and twenty degrees of frost. I'm fond of the winter; I'm fond of it because at that time, even in the hardest frosts, it's particularly snug at home. It's pleasant to put on one's fur jacket and felt overboots on a clear frosty day, to do something in the garden or in the yard, or to read in a well warmed room, to sit in my father's study before the open fire, to wash in my country bath-house.

. . . Only if there is no mother in the house, no sister and no children, it is somehow dreary on winter evenings, and they seem extraordinarily long and quiet. And the warmer and snugger it is, the more acutely is this lack felt. In the winter when I came back from abroad, the evenings were endlessly long, I was intensely depressed, so depressed that I could not even read; in the daytime I was coming and going, clearing away the snow in the garden or feeding the chickens and the calves, but in the evening it was all up with me.

I had never cared for visitors before, but now I was glad of them, for I knew there was sure to be talk of Ariadne. Kotlovitch, the spiritualist, used often to come to talk about his sister, and sometimes he brought with him his friend Prince Maktuev, who was as much in love with Ariadne as I was. To sit in Ariadne's room, to finger the keys of her piano, to look at her music was a necessity for the prince—he could not live without it; and the spirit of his grandfather Ilarion was still predicting that sooner or later she would be his wife. The prince usually stayed a long time with us, from lunch to midnight, saying nothing all the time; in silence he would drink two or three bottles of beer, and from time to time, to show that he too was taking part in the conversation, he would laugh an abrupt, melancholy, foolish laugh. Before going home he would always take me aside and ask me in an undertone: "When did you see Ariadne Grigoryevna last? Was she quite well? I suppose she's not tired of being out there?"

Spring came on. There was the harrowing to do and then the sowing of spring corn and clover. I was sad, but there was the feeling of spring. One longed to accept the inevitable. Working in the fields and listening to the larks, I asked myself: "Couldn't I have done with this question of personal happiness once and for all? Couldn't I lay aside my fancy and marry a simple peasant girl?"

Suddenly when we were at our very busiest, I got a letter with the Italian stamp, and the clover and the beehives and the calves and the peasant girl all floated away like smoke. This time Ariadne wrote that she was profoundly, infinitely unhappy. She reproached me for not holding out a helping hand to her, for looking down upon her from the heights of my virtue and deserting her at the moment of danger. All this was written in a large, nervous handwriting with blots and smudges, and it was evident that she wrote in haste and distress. In conclusion she besought me to come and save her. Again my anchor was hauled up and I was carried away. Ariadne was in Rome. I arrived late in the evening, and when she saw me, she sobbed and threw herself on my neck. She had not changed at all that winter, and was just as young and charming. We had supper together and afterwards drove about Rome until dawn, and all the time she kept telling me about her doings. I asked where Lubkov was.

"Don't remind me of that creature!" she cried. "He is loathsome and disgusting to me!"

"But I thought you loved him," I said.

"Never," she said. "At first he struck me as original and aroused my pity, that was all. He is insolent and takes a woman by storm. And that's attractive. But we won't talk about him. That is a melancholy page in my life. He has gone to Russia to get money. Serve him right! I told him not to dare to come back."

She was living then, not at an hotel, but in a private lodging of two rooms which she had decorated in her own taste, frigidly and luxuriously.

After Lubkov had gone away she had borrowed from her acquaintances about five thousand francs, and my arrival certainly was the one salvation for her.

I had reckoned on taking her back to the country, but I did not succeed in that. She was homesick for her native place, but her recollections of the poverty she had been through there, of privations, of the rusty roof on her brother's house, roused a shudder of disgust, and when I suggested going home to her, she squeezed my hands convulsively and said:

"No, no, I shall die of boredom there!"

Then my love entered upon its final phase.

"Be the darling that you used to be; love me a little," said Ariadne, bending over to me. "You're sulky and prudent, you're afraid to yield to impulse, and keep thinking of consequences, and that's dull. Come, I beg you, I beseech you, be nice to me! . . . My pure one, my holy one, my dear one, I love you so!"

I became her lover. For a month anyway I was like a madman, conscious of nothing but rapture. To hold in one's arms a young and lovely body, with bliss to feel her warmth every time one waked up from sleep, and to remember that she was there—she, my Ariadne!—oh, it was not easy to get used to that! But yet I did get used to it, and by degrees became capable of reflecting on my new position. First of all, I realised, as before, that Ariadne did not love me. But she wanted to be really in love, she was afraid of solitude, and, above all, I was healthy, young, vigorous; she was sensual, like all cold people, as a rule—and we both made a show of being united by a passionate, mutual love. Afterwards I realised something else, too.

We stayed in Rome, in Naples, in Florence; we went to Paris, but there we thought it cold and went back to Italy. We introduced ourselves everywhere as husband and wife, wealthy landowners. People readily made our acquaintance and Ariadne had great social success everywhere. As she took lessons in painting, she was called an artist, and only imagine, that quite suited her, though she had not the slightest trace of talent.

She would sleep every day till two or three o'clock; she had her coffee and lunch in bed. At dinner she would eat soup, lobster, fish, meat, asparagus, game, and after she had gone to bed I used to bring up something, for instance roast beef, and she would eat it with a melancholy, careworn expression, and if she waked in the night she would eat apples and oranges.

The chief, so to say fundamental, characteristic of the woman was an amazing duplicity. She was continually deceitful every minute, apparently apart from any necessity, as it were by instinct, by an impulse such as makes the sparrow chirrup and the cockroach waggle its antennæ. She was deceitful with me, with the footman, with the porter, with the tradesmen in the shops, with her acquaintances; not one conversation, not one meeting, took place without affectation and pretence. A man had only to come into our room—whoever it might be, a waiter, or a baron—for her eyes, her expression, her voice to change, even the contour of her figure was transformed. At the very first glance at her then, you would have said there were no more wealthy and fashionable people in Italy than we. She never met an artist or a musician without telling him all sorts of lies about his remarkable talent.

"You have such a talent!" she would say, in honeyed cadences, "I'm really afraid of you. I think you must see right through people."

And all this simply in order to please, to be successful, to be fascinating! She waked up every morning with the one thought of "pleasing"! It was the aim and object of her life. If I had told her that in such a house, in such a street, there lived a man who was not attracted by her, it would have caused her real suffering. She wanted every day to enchant, to captivate, to drive men crazy. The fact that I was in her power and reduced to a complete nonentity before her charms gave her the same sort of satisfaction that visitors used to feel in tournaments. My subjection was not enough, and at nights, stretched out like a tigress, uncovered—she was always too hot—she would read the letters sent her by Lubkov; he besought her to return to Russia, vowing if she did not he would rob or murder some one to get the money to come to her. She hated him, but his passionate, slavish letters excited her. She had an extraordinary opinion of her own charms; she imagined that if somewhere, in some great assembly, men could have seen how beautifully she was made and the colour of her skin, she would have vanquished all Italy, the whole world. Her talk of her figure, of her skin, offended me, and observing this, she would, when she was angry, to vex me, say all sorts of vulgar things, taunting me. One day when we were at the summer villa of a lady of our acquaintance, and she lost her temper, she even went so far as to say: "If you don't leave off boring me with your sermons, I'll undress this minute and lie naked here on these flowers."

Often looking at her asleep, or eating, or trying to assume a naïve expression, I wondered why that extraordinary beauty, grace, and intelligence had been given her by God. Could it simply be for lolling in bed, eating and lying, lying endlessly? And was she intelligent really? She was afraid of three candles in a row, of the number thirteen, was terrified of spells and bad dreams. She argued about free love and freedom in general like a bigoted old woman, declared that Boleslav Markevitch was a better writer than Turgenev. But she was diabolically cunning and sharp, and knew how to seem a highly educated, advanced person in company.

Even at a good-humoured moment, she could always insult a servant or kill an insect without a pang; she liked bull-fights, liked to read about murders, and was angry when prisoners were acquitted.

For the life Ariadne and I were leading, we had to have a great deal of money. My poor father sent me his pension, all the little sums he received, borrowed for me wherever he could, and when one day he answered me: "Non habeo," I sent him a desperate telegram in which I besought him to mortgage the estate. A little later I begged him to get money somehow on a second mortgage. He did this too without a murmur and sent me every farthing. Ariadne despised the practical side of life; all this was no concern of hers, and when flinging away thousands of francs to satisfy her mad desires I groaned like an old tree, she would be singing "Addio bella Napoli" with a light heart.

Little by little I grew cold to her and began to be ashamed of our tie. I am not fond of pregnancy and confinements, but now I sometimes dreamed of a child who would have been at least a formal justification of our life. That I might not be completely disgusted with myself, I began reading and visiting museums and galleries, gave up drinking and took to eating very little. If one keeps oneself well in hand from morning to night, one's heart seems lighter. I began to bore Ariadne too. The people with whom she won her triumphs were, by the way, all of the middling sort; as before, there were no ambassadors, there was no salon, the money did not run to it, and this mortified her and made her sob, and she announced to me at last that perhaps she would not be against our returning to Russia.

And here we are on our way. For the last few months she has been zealously corresponding with her brother; she evidently has some secret projects, but what they are—God knows! I am sick of trying to fathom her underhand schemes! But we're going, not to the country, but to Yalta and afterwards to the Caucasus. She can only exist now at watering-places, and if you knew how I hate all these watering-places, how suffocated and ashamed I am in them. If I could be in the country now! If I could only be working now, earning my bread by the sweat of my brow, atoning for my follies. I am conscious of a superabundance of energy and I believe that if I were to put that energy to work I could redeem my estate in five years. But now, as you see, there is a complication. Here we're not abroad, but in mother Russia; we shall have to think of lawful wedlock. Of course, all attraction is over; there is no trace left of my old love, but, however that may be, I am bound in honour to marry her.

• • •

Shamohin, excited by his story, went below with me and we continued talking about women. It was late. It appeared that he and I were in the same cabin.

"So far it is only in the village that woman has not fallen behind man," said Shamohin. "There she thinks and feels just as man does, and struggles with nature in the name of culture as zealously as he. In the towns the woman of the bourgeois or intellectual class has long since fallen behind, and is returning to her primitive condition. She is half a human beast already, and, thanks to her, a great deal of what had been won by human genius has been lost again; the woman gradually disappears and in her place is the primitive female. This dropping-back on the part of the educated woman is a real danger to culture; in her retrogressive movement she tries to drag man after her and prevents him from moving forward. That is incontestable."

I asked: "Why generalise? Why judge of all women from Ariadne alone?The very struggle of women for education and sexual equality, whichI look upon as a struggle for justice, precludes any hypothesis ofa retrograde movement."

But Shamohin scarcely listened to me and he smiled distrustfully. He was a passionate, convinced misogynist, and it was impossible to alter his convictions.

"Oh, nonsense!" he interrupted. "When once a woman sees in me, not a man, not an equal, but a male, and her one anxiety all her life is to attract me—that is, to take possession of me—how can one talk of their rights? Oh, don't you believe them; they are very, very cunning! We men make a great stir about their emancipation, but they don't care about their emancipation at all, they only pretend to care about it; they are horribly cunning things, horribly cunning!"

I began to feel sleepy and weary of discussion. I turned over with my face to the wall.

"Yes," I heard as I fell asleep—"yes, and it's our education that's at fault, sir. In our towns, the whole education and bringing up of women in its essence tends to develop her into the human beast — that is, to make her attractive to the male and able to vanquish him. Yes, indeed"—Shamohiri sighed—"little girls ought to be taught and brought up with boys, so that they might be always together. A woman ought to be trained so that she may be able, like a man, to recognise when she's wrong, or she always thinks she's in the right. Instil into a little girl from her cradle that a man is not first of all a cavalier or a possible lover, but her neighbour, her equal in everything. Train her to think logically, to generalise, and do not assure her that her brain weighs less than a man's and that therefore she can be indifferent to the sciences, to the arts, to the tasks of culture in general. The apprentice to the shoemaker or the house painter has a brain of smaller size than the grown-up man too, yet he works, suffers, takes his part in the general struggle for existence. We must give up our attitude to the physiological aspect, too—to pregnancy and childbirth, seeing that in the first place women don't have babies every month; secondly, not all women have babies; and, thirdly, a normal countrywoman works in the fields up to the day of her confinement and it does her no harm. Then there ought to be absolute equality in everyday life. If a man gives a lady his chair or picks up the handkerchief she has dropped, let her repay him in the same way. I have no objection if a girl of good family helps me to put on my coat or hands me a glass of water—"

I heard no more, for I fell asleep.

Next morning when we were approaching Sevastopol, it was damp, unpleasant weather; the ship rocked. Shamohin sat on deck with me, brooding and silent. When the bell rang for tea, men with their coat-collars turned up and ladies with pale, sleepy faces began going below; a young and very beautiful lady, the one who had been so angry with the Customs officers at Volotchisk, stopped before Shamohin and said with the expression of a naughty, fretful child:

"Jean, your birdie's been sea-sick."

Afterwards when I was at Yalta I saw the same beautiful lady dashing about on horseback with a couple of officers hardly able to keep up with her. And one morning I saw her in an overall and a Phrygian cap, sketching on the sea-front with a great crowd admiring her a little way off. I too was introduced to her. She pressed my hand with great warmth, and looking at me ecstatically, thanked me in honeyed cadences for the pleasure I had given her by my writings.

"Don't you believe her," Shamohin whispered to me, "she has never read a word of them."

When I was walking on the sea-front in the early evening Shamohin met me with his arms full of big parcels of fruits and dainties.

"Prince Maktuev is here!" he said joyfully. "He came yesterday with her brother, the spiritualist! Now I understand what she was writing to him about! Oh, Lord!" he went on, gazing up to heaven, and pressing his parcels to his bosom. "If she hits it off with the prince, it means freedom, then I can go back to the country with my father!"

And he ran on.

"I begin to believe in spirits," he called to me, looking back. "The spirit of grandfather Ilarion seems to have prophesied the truth! Oh, if only it is so!"

• • •

The day after this meeting I left Yalta and how Shamohin's story ended I don't know.

NOTES

Max Nordau: Max Simon Nordau (1848-1923) was a Hungarian philosopher

Raphael's Madonna: Raphael (1483-1520) painted many madonnas

novel of Weltmann's: A. F. Weltmann (1800-1870) was a minor Russian novelist

reddish agarics: mushrooms

homeopathy: a pseudoscience that treats disease by administering minute doses of drugs that in massive amounts produce symptoms in healthy individuals similar to the disease itself

Cæsar's wife: Julius Cæsar (c. 102 B. C. - 44 B. C.); the wife of a dictator is very powerful

char-à-banc: bus (horse-drawn)

kvass: a Russian beer made from rye or barley

dépendance: an outbuilding

comme il faut: proper, decent

guldens: Austrian coins worth at the time of the story about 1 ruble

café complet: coffee with rolls, butter, and jam

enter into the position: she won't understand my position

twenty degrees of frost: 13 below zero F.

three candles in a row: Russians place three candles next to a coffin, so three candles are a sign of a death in the family

Boleslav Markevitch: Boleslav M. Markevitch (1822-1884) was a minor novelist who was also extremely conservative politically

Non habeo: I have none

TERROR
MY FRIEND'S STORY

Dmitri Petrovich Silin had taken his degree and entered the government service in Petersburg, but at thirty he gave up his post and went in for agriculture. His farming was fairly successful, and yet it always seemed to me that he was not in his proper place, and that he would do well to go back to Petersburg. When sunburnt, grey with dust, exhausted with toil, he met me near the gates or at the entrance, and then at supper struggled with sleepiness and his wife took him off to bed as though he were a baby; or when, overcoming his sleepiness, he began in his soft, cordial, almost imploring voice, to talk about his really excellent ideas, I saw him not as a farmer nor an agriculturist, but only as a worried and exhausted man, and it was clear to me that he did not really care for farming, but that all he wanted was for the day to be over and "Thank God for it."

I liked to be with him, and I used to stay on his farm for two or three days at a time. I liked his house, and his park, and his big fruit garden, and the river—and his philosophy, which was clear, though rather spiritless and rhetorical. I suppose I was fond of him on his own account, though I can't say that for certain, as I have not up to now succeeded in analysing my feelings at that time. He was an intelligent, kind-hearted, genuine man, and not a bore, but I remember that when he confided to me his most treasured secrets and spoke of our relation to each other as friendship, it disturbed me unpleasantly, and I was conscious of awkwardness. In his affection for me there was something inappropriate, tiresome, and I should have greatly preferred commonplace friendly relations.

The fact is that I was extremely attracted by his wife, Marya Sergeyevna. I was not in love with her, but I was attracted by her face, her eyes, her voice, her walk. I missed her when I did not see her for a long time, and my imagination pictured no one at that time so eagerly as that young, beautiful, elegant woman. I had no definite designs in regard to her, and did not dream of anything of the sort, yet for some reason, whenever we were left alone, I remembered that her husband looked upon me as his friend, and I felt awkward. When she played my favourite pieces on the piano or told me something interesting, I listened with pleasure, and yet at the same time for some reason the reflection that she loved her husband, that he was my friend, and that she herself looked upon me as his friend, obtruded themselves upon me, my spirits flagged, and I became listless, awkward, and dull. She noticed this change and would usually say:

"You are dull without your friend. We must send out to the fields for him."

And when Dmitri Petrovitch came in, she would say:

"Well, here is your friend now. Rejoice."

So passed a year and a half.

It somehow happened one July Sunday that Dmitri Petrovitch and I, having nothing to do, drove to the big village of Klushino to buy things for supper. While we were going from one shop to another the sun set and the evening came on—the evening which I shall probably never forget in my life. After buying cheese that smelt like soap, and petrified sausages that smelt of tar, we went to the tavern to ask whether they had any beer. Our coachman went off to the blacksmith to get our horses shod, and we told him we would wait for him near the church. We walked, talked, laughed over our purchases, while a man who was known in the district by a very strange nickname, "Forty Martyrs," followed us all the while in silence with a mysterious air like a detective. This Forty Martyrs was no other than Gavril Syeverov, or more simply Gavryushka, who had been for a short time in my service as a footman and had been dismissed by me for drunkenness. He had been in Dmitri Petrovitch's service, too, and by him had been dismissed for the same vice. He was an inveterate drunkard, and indeed his whole life was as drunk and disorderly as himself. His father had been a priest and his mother of noble rank, so by birth he belonged to the privileged class; but however carefully I scrutinized his exhausted, respectful, and always perspiring face, his red beard now turning grey, his pitifully torn reefer jacket and his red shirt, I could not discover in him the faintest trace of anything we associate with privilege. He spoke of himself as a man of education, and used to say that he had been in a clerical school, but had not finished his studies there, as he had been expelled for smoking; then he had sung in the bishop's choir and lived for two years in a monastery, from which he was also expelled, but this time not for smoking but for "his weakness." He had walked all over two provinces, had presented petitions to the Consistory, and to various government offices, and had been four times on his trial. At last, being stranded in our district, he had served as a footman, as a forester, as a kennelman, as a sexton, had married a cook who was a widow and rather a loose character, and had so hopelessly sunk into a menial position, and had grown so used to filth and dirt, that he even spoke of his privileged origin with a certain scepticism, as of some myth. At the time I am describing, he was hanging about without a job, calling himself a carrier and a huntsman, and his wife had disappeared and made no sign.

From the tavern we went to the church and sat in the porch, waiting for the coachman. Forty Martyrs stood a little way off and put his hand before his mouth in order to cough in it respectfully if need be. By now it was dark; there was a strong smell of evening dampness, and the moon was on the point of rising. There were only two clouds in the clear starry sky exactly over our heads: one big one and one smaller; alone in the sky they were racing after one another like mother and child, in the direction where the sunset was glowing.

"What a glorious day!" said Dmitri Petrovitch.

"In the extreme . . ." Forty Martyrs assented, and he coughed respectfully into his hand. "How was it, Dmitri Petrovitch, you thought to visit these parts?" he asked in an ingratiating voice, evidently anxious to get up a conversation.

Dmitri Petrovitch made no answer. Forty Martyrs heaved a deep sigh and said softly, not looking at us:

"I suffer solely through a cause to which I must answer to Almighty God. No doubt about it, I am a hopeless and incompetent man; but believe me, on my conscience, I am without a crust of bread and worse off than a dog. . . . Forgive me, Dmitri Petrovitch."

Silin was not listening, but sat musing with his head propped on his fists. The church stood at the end of the street on the high riverbank, and through the trellis gate of the enclosure we could see the river, the water-meadows on the near side of it, and the crimson glare of a camp fire about which black figures of men and horses were moving. And beyond the fire, further away, there were other lights, where there was a little village. They were singing there. On the river, and here and there on the meadows, a mist was rising. High narrow coils of mist, thick and white as milk, were trailing over the river, hiding the reflection of the stars and hovering over the willows. Every minute they changed their form, and it seemed as though some were embracing, others were bowing, others lifting up their arms to heaven with wide sleeves like priests, as though they were praying. . . .

Probably they reminded Dmitri Petrovitch of ghosts and of the dead, for he turned facing me and asked with a mournful smile:

"Tell me, my dear fellow, why is it that when we want to tell some terrible, mysterious, and fantastic story, we draw our material, not from life, but invariably from the world of ghosts and of the shadows beyond the grave."

"We are frightened of what we don't understand."

"And do you understand life? Tell me: do you understand life better than the world beyond the grave?"

Dmitri Petrovitch was sitting quite close to me, so that I felt his breath upon my cheek. In the evening twilight his pale, lean face seemed paler than ever and his dark beard was black as soot. His eyes were sad, truthful, and a little frightened, as though he were about to tell me something horrible. He looked into my eyes and went on in his habitual imploring voice:

"Our life and the life beyond the grave are equally incomprehensible and horrible. If any one is afraid of ghosts he ought to be afraid, too, of me, and of those lights and of the sky, seeing that, if you come to reflect, all that is no less fantastic and beyond our grasp than apparitions from the other world. Prince Hamlet did not kill himself because he was afraid of the visions that might haunt his dreams after death. I like that famous soliloquy of his, but, to be candid, it never touched my soul. I will confess to you as a friend that in moments of depression I have sometimes pictured to myself the hour of my death. My fancy invented thousands of the gloomiest visions, and I have succeeded in working myself up to an agonizing exaltation, to a state of nightmare, and I assure you that that did not seem to me more terrible than reality. What I mean is, apparitions are terrible, but life is terrible, too. I don't understand life and I am afraid of it, my dear boy; I don't know. Perhaps I am a morbid person, unhinged. It seems to a sound, healthy man that he understands everything he sees and hears, but that 'seeming' is lost to me, and from day to day I am poisoning myself with terror. There is a disease, the fear of open spaces, but my disease is the fear of life. When I lie on the grass and watch a little beetle which was born yesterday and understands nothing, it seems to me that its life consists of nothing else but fear, and in it I see myself."

"What is it exactly you are frightened of?" I asked.

"I am afraid of everything. I am not by nature a profound thinker, and I take little interest in such questions as the life beyond the grave, the destiny of humanity, and, in fact, I am rarely carried away to the heights. What chiefly frightens me is the common routine of life from which none of us can escape. I am incapable of distinguishing what is true and what is false in my actions, and they worry me. I recognize that education and the conditions of life have imprisoned me in a narrow circle of falsity, that my whole life is nothing else than a daily effort to deceive myself and other people, and to avoid noticing it; and I am frightened at the thought that to the day of my death I shall not escape from this falsity. To-day I do something and to-morrow I do not understand why I did it. I entered the service in Petersburg and took fright; I came here to work on the land, and here, too, I am frightened. . . . I see that we know very little and so make mistakes every day. We are unjust, we slander one another and spoil each other's lives, we waste all our powers on trash which we do not need and which hinders us from living; and that frightens me, because I don't understand why and for whom it is necessary. I don't understand men, my dear fellow, and I am afraid of them. It frightens me to look at the peasants, and I don't know for what higher objects they are suffering and what they are living for. If life is an enjoyment, then they are unnecessary, superfluous people; if the object and meaning of life is to be found in poverty and unending, hopeless ignorance, I can't understand for whom and what this torture is necessary. I understand no one and nothing. Kindly try to understand this specimen, for instance," said Dmitri Petrovitch, pointing to Forty Martyrs. "Think of him!"

Noticing that we were looking at him, Forty Martyrs coughed deferentially into his fist and said:

"I was always a faithful servant with good masters, but the great trouble has been spirituous liquor. If a poor fellow like me were shown consideration and given a place, I would kiss the ikon. My word's my bond."

The sexton walked by, looked at us in amazement, and began pulling the rope. The bell, abruptly breaking upon the stillness of the evening, struck ten with a slow and prolonged note.

"It's ten o'clock, though," said Dmitri Petrovitch. "It's time we were going. Yes, my dear fellow," he sighed, "if only you knew how afraid I am of my ordinary everyday thoughts, in which one would have thought there should be nothing dreadful. To prevent myself thinking I distract my mind with work and try to tire myself out that I may sleep sound at night. Children, a wife—all that seems ordinary with other people; but how that weighs upon me, my dear fellow!"

He rubbed his face with his hands, cleared his throat, and laughed.

"If I could only tell you how I have played the fool in my life!" he said. "They all tell me that I have a sweet wife, charming children, and that I am a good husband and father. They think I am very happy and envy me. But since it has come to that, I will tell you in secret: my happy family life is only a grievous misunderstanding, and I am afraid of it." His pale face was distorted by a wry smile. He put his arm round my waist and went on in an undertone:

"You are my true friend; I believe in you and have a deep respect for you. Heaven gave us friendship that we may open our hearts and escape from the secrets that weigh upon us. Let me take advantage of your friendly feeling for me and tell you the whole truth. My home life, which seems to you so enchanting, is my chief misery and my chief terror. I got married in a strange and stupid way. I must tell you that I was madly in love with Masha before I married her, and was courting her for two years. I asked her to marry me five times, and she refused me because she did not care for me in the least. The sixth, when burning with passion I crawled on my knees before her and implored her to take a beggar and marry me, she consented. . . . What she said to me was: 'I don't love you, but I will be true to you. . . .' I accepted that condition with rapture. At the time I understood what that meant, but I swear to God I don't understand it now. 'I don't love you, but I will be true to you.' What does that mean? It's a fog, a darkness. I love her now as intensely as I did the day we were married, while she, I believe, is as indifferent as ever, and I believe she is glad when I go away from home. I don't know for certain whether she cares for me or not —I don't know, I don't know; but, as you see, we live under the same roof, call each other 'thou,' sleep together, have children, our property is in common. . . . What does it mean, what does it mean? What is the object of it? And do you understand it at all, my dear fellow? It's cruel torture! Because I don't understand our relations, I hate, sometimes her, sometimes myself, sometimes both at once. Everything is in a tangle in my brain; I torment myself and grow stupid. And as though to spite me, she grows more beautiful every day, she is getting more wonderful. . . I fancy her hair is marvellous, and her smile is like no other woman's. I love her, and I know that my love is hopeless. Hopeless love for a woman by whom one has two children! Is that intelligible? And isn't it terrible? Isn't it more terrible than ghosts?"

He was in the mood to have talked on a good deal longer, but luckily we heard the coachman's voice. Our horses had arrived. We got into the carriage, and Forty Martyrs, taking off his cap, helped us both into the carriage with an expression that suggested that he had long been waiting for an opportunity to come in contact with our precious persons.

"Dmitri Petrovitch, let me come to you," he said, blinking furiously and tilting his head on one side. "Show divine mercy! I am dying of hunger!"

"Very well," said Silin. "Come, you shall stay three days, and then we shall see."

"Certainly, sir," said Forty Martyrs, overjoyed. "I'll come today, sir."

It was a five miles' drive home. Dmitri Petrovitch, glad that he had at last opened his heart to his friend, kept his arm round my waist all the way; and speaking now, not with bitterness and not with apprehension, but quite cheerfully, told me that if everything had been satisfactory in his home life, he should have returned to Petersburg and taken up scientific work there. The movement which had driven so many gifted young men into the country was, he said, a deplorable movement. We had plenty of rye and wheat in Russia, but absolutely no cultured people. The strong and gifted among the young ought to take up science, art, and politics; to act otherwise meant being wasteful. He generalized with pleasure and expressed regret that he would be parting from me early next morning, as he had to go to a sale of timber.

And I felt awkward and depressed, and it seemed to me that I was deceiving the man. And at the same time it was pleasant to me. I gazed at the immense crimson moon which was rising, and pictured the tall, graceful, fair woman, with her pale face, always well-dressed and fragrant with some special scent, rather like musk, and for some reason it pleased me to think she did not love her husband.

On reaching home, we sat down to supper. Marya Sergeyevna, laughing, regaled us with our purchases, and I thought that she certainly had wonderful hair and that her smile was unlike any other woman's. I watched her, and I wanted to detect in every look and movement that she did not love her husband, and I fancied that I did see it.

Dmitri Petrovitch was soon struggling with sleep. After supper he sat with us for ten minutes and said:

"Do as you please, my friends, but I have to be up at three o'clock tomorrow morning. Excuse my leaving you."

He kissed his wife tenderly, pressed my hand with warmth and gratitude, and made me promise that I would certainly come the following week. That he might not oversleep next morning, he went to spend the night in the lodge.

Marya Sergeyevna always sat up late, in the Petersburg fashion, and for some reason on this occasion I was glad of it.

"And now," I began when we were left alone, "and now you'll be kind and play me something."

I felt no desire for music, but I did not know how to begin the conversation. She sat down to the piano and played, I don't remember what. I sat down beside her and looked at her plump white hands and tried to read something on her cold, indifferent face. Then she smiled at something and looked at me.

"You are dull without your friend," she said.

I laughed.

"It would be enough for friendship to be here once a month, but I turn up oftener than once a week."

Saying this, I got up and walked from one end of the room to the other. She too got up and walked away to the fireplace.

"What do you mean to say by that?" she said, raising her large, clear eyes and looking at me.

I made no answer.

"What you say is not true," she went on, after a moment's thought. "You only come here on account of Dmitri Petrovitch. Well, I am very glad. One does not often see such friendships nowadays."

"Aha!" I thought, and, not knowing what to say, I asked: "Would you care for a turn in the garden?"

I went out upon the verandah. Nervous shudders were running over my head and I felt chilly with excitement. I was convinced now that our conversation would be utterly trivial, and that there was nothing particular we should be able to say to one another, but that, that night, what I did not dare to dream of was bound to happen—that it was bound to be that night or never.

"What lovely weather!" I said aloud.

"It makes absolutely no difference to me," she answered.

I went into the drawing-room. Marya Sergeyevna was standing, as before, near the fireplace, with her hands behind her back, looking away and thinking of something.

"Why does it make no difference to you?" I asked.

"Because I am bored. You are only bored without your friend, but I am always bored. However . . . that is of no interest to you."

I sat down to the piano and struck a few chords, waiting to hear what she would say.

"Please don't stand on ceremony," she said, looking angrily at me, and she seemed as though on the point of crying with vexation. "If you are sleepy, go to bed. Because you are Dmitri Petrovitch's friend, you are not in duty bound to be bored with his wife's company. I don't want a sacrifice. Please go."

I did not, of course, go to bed. She went out on the verandah while I remained in the drawing-room and spent five minutes turning over the music. Then I went out, too. We stood close together in the shadow of the curtains, and below us were the steps bathed in moonlight. The black shadows of the trees stretched across the flower beds and the yellow sand of the paths.

"I shall have to go away tomorrow, too," I said.

"Of course, if my husband's not at home you can't stay here," she said sarcastically. "I can imagine how miserable you would be if you were in love with me! Wait a bit: one day I shall throw myself on your neck. . . . I shall see with what horror you will run away from me. That would be interesting."

Her words and her pale face were angry, but her eyes were full of tender passionate love. I already looked upon this lovely creature as my property, and then for the first time I noticed that she had golden eyebrows, exquisite eyebrows. I had never seen such eyebrows before. The thought that I might at once press her to my heart, caress her, touch her wonderful hair, seemed to me such a miracle that I laughed and shut my eyes.

"It's bed-time now. . . . A peaceful night," she said.

"I don't want a peaceful night," I said, laughing, following her into the drawing-room. "I shall curse this night if it is a peaceful one."

Pressing her hand, and escorting her to the door, I saw by her face that she understood me, and was glad that I understood her, too.

I went to my room. Near the books on the table lay Dmitri Petrovitch's cap, and that reminded me of his affection for me. I took my stick and went out into the garden. The mist had risen here, too, and the same tall, narrow, ghostly shapes which I had seen earlier on the river were trailing round the trees and bushes and wrapping about them. What a pity I could not talk to them!

In the extraordinarily transparent air, each leaf, each drop of dew stood out distinctly; it was all smiling at me in the stillness half asleep, and as I passed the green seats I recalled the words in some play of Shakespeare's: "How sweetly falls the moonlight on yon seat!"

There was a mound in the garden; I went up it and sat down. I was tormented by a delicious feeling. I knew for certain that in a moment I should hold in my arms, should press to my heart her magnificent body, should kiss her golden eyebrows; and I wanted to disbelieve it, to tantalize myself, and was sorry that she had cost me so little trouble and had yielded so soon.

But suddenly I heard heavy footsteps. A man of medium height appeared in the avenue, and I recognized him at once as Forty Martyrs. He sat down on the bench and heaved a deep sigh, then crossed himself three times and lay down. A minute later he got up and lay on the other side. The gnats and the dampness of the night prevented his sleeping.

"Oh, life!" he said. "Wretched, bitter life!"

Looking at his bent, wasted body and hearing his heavy, noisy sighs, I thought of an unhappy, bitter life of which the confession had been made to me that day, and I felt uneasy and frightened at my blissful mood. I came down the knoll and went to the house.

"Life, as he thinks, is terrible," I thought, "so don't stand on ceremony with it, bend it to your will, and until it crushes you, snatch all you can wring from it."

Marya Sergeyevna was standing on the verandah. I put my arms round her without a word, and began greedily kissing her eyebrows, her temples, her neck. . . .

In my room she told me she had loved me for a long time, more than a year. She vowed eternal love, cried and begged me to take her away with me. I repeatedly took her to the window to look at her face in the moonlight, and she seemed to me a lovely dream, and I made haste to hold her tight to convince myself of the truth of it. It was long since I had known such raptures. . . . Yet somewhere far away at the bottom of my heart I felt an awkwardness, and I was ill at ease. In her love for me there was something incongruous and burdensome, just as in Dmitri Petrovitch's friendship. It was a great, serious passion with tears and vows, and I wanted nothing serious in it—no tears, no vows, no talk of the future. Let that moonlight night flash through our lives like a meteor and—basta!

At three o'clock she went out of my room, and, while I was standing in the doorway, looking after her, at the end of the corridor Dmitri Petrovitch suddenly made his appearance; she started and stood aside to let him pass, and her whole figure was expressive of repulsion. He gave a strange smile, coughed, and came into my room.

"I forgot my cap here yesterday," he said without looking at me.

He found it and, holding it in both hands, put it on his head; then he looked at my confused face, at my slippers, and said in a strange, husky voice unlike his own:

"I suppose it must be my fate that I should understand nothing. . . . If you understand anything, I congratulate you. It's all darkness before my eyes."

And he went out, clearing his throat. Afterwards from the window I saw him by the stable, harnessing the horses with his own hands. His hands were trembling, he was in nervous haste and kept looking round at the house; probably he was feeling terror. Then he got into the gig, and, with a strange expression as though afraid of being pursued, lashed the horses.

Shortly afterwards I set off, too. The sun was already rising, and the mist of the previous day clung timidly to the bushes and the hillocks. On the box of the carriage was sitting Forty Martyrs; he had already succeeded in getting drunk and was muttering tipsy nonsense.

"I am a free man," he shouted to the horses. "Ah, my honeys, I am a nobleman in my own right, if you care to know!"

The terror of Dmitri Petrovitch, the thought of whom I could not get out of my head, infected me. I thought of what had happened and could make nothing of it. I looked at the rooks, and it seemed so strange and terrible that they were flying.

"Why have I done this?" I kept asking myself in bewilderment and despair. "Why has it turned out like this and not differently? To whom and for what was it necessary that she should love me in earnest, and that he should come into my room to fetch his cap? What had a cap to do with it?"

I set off for Petersburg that day, and I have not seen Dmitri Petrovitch nor his wife since. I am told that they are still living together.

NOTES

privileged class: he only qualifies as a "hereditary honorary citizen," not a gentleman, although he is still a step above peasants and other members of the lower classes

Prince Hamlet: Hamlet, III,2, 66-68; part of the famous "To be or not to be" soliloquy

thou: use the intimate form of "you" which Russians use with children, close relatives, and pets

yon seat: Russian slight mistranslation of "How sweet the moonlight sleeps upon this bank!" The Merchant of Venice, V, 1, 54

basta!: stop it; enough

A PROBLEM

The strictest measures were taken that the Uskovs' family secret might not leak out and become generally known. Half of the servants were sent off to the theatre or the circus; the other half were sitting in the kitchen and not allowed to leave it. Orders were given that no one was to be admitted. The wife of the Colonel, her sister, and the governess, though they had been initiated into the secret, kept up a pretence of knowing nothing; they sat in the dining-room and did not show themselves in the drawing-room or the hall.

Sasha Uskov, the young man of twenty-five who was the cause of all the commotion, had arrived some time before, and by the advice of kind-hearted Ivan Markovitch, his uncle, who was taking his part, he sat meekly in the hall by the door leading to the study, and prepared himself to make an open, candid explanation.

The other side of the door, in the study, a family council was being held. The subject under discussion was an exceedingly disagreeable and delicate one. Sasha Uskov had cashed at one of the banks a false promissory note, and it had become due for payment three days before, and now his two paternal uncles and Ivan Markovitch, the brother of his dead mother, were deciding the question whether they should pay the money and save the family honour, or wash their hands of it and leave the case to go for trial.

To outsiders who have no personal interest in the matter such questions seem simple; for those who are so unfortunate as to have to decide them in earnest they are extremely difficult. The uncles had been talking for a long time, but the problem seemed no nearer decision.

"My friends!" said the uncle who was a colonel, and there was a note of exhaustion and bitterness in his voice. "Who says that family honour is a mere convention? I don't say that at all. I am only warning you against a false view; I am pointing out the possibility of an unpardonable mistake. How can you fail to see it? I am not speaking Chinese; I am speaking Russian!"

"My dear fellow, we do understand," Ivan Markovitch protested mildly.

"How can you understand if you say that I don't believe in family honour? I repeat once more: fa-mil-y ho-nour fal-sely un-der-stood is a prejudice! Falsely understood! That's what I say: whatever may be the motives for screening a scoundrel, whoever he may be, and helping him to escape punishment, it is contrary to law and unworthy of a gentleman. It's not saving the family honour; it's civic cowardice! Take the army, for instance. . . . The honour of the army is more precious to us than any other honour, yet we don't screen our guilty members, but condemn them. And does the honour of the army suffer in consequence? Quite the opposite!"

The other paternal uncle, an official in the Treasury, a taciturn, dull-witted, and rheumatic man, sat silent, or spoke only of the fact that the Uskovs' name would get into the newspapers if the case went for trial. His opinion was that the case ought to be hushed up from the first and not become public property; but, apart from publicity in the newspapers, he advanced no other argument in support of this opinion.

The maternal uncle, kind-hearted Ivan Markovitch, spoke smoothly, softly, and with a tremor in his voice. He began with saying that youth has its rights and its peculiar temptations. Which of us has not been young, and who has not been led astray? To say nothing of ordinary mortals, even great men have not escaped errors and mistakes in their youth. Take, for instance, the biography of great writers. Did not every one of them gamble, drink, and draw down upon himself the anger of right-thinking people in his young days? If Sasha's error bordered upon crime, they must remember that Sasha had received practically no education; he had been expelled from the high school in the fifth class; he had lost his parents in early childhood, and so had been left at the tenderest age without guidance and good, benevolent influences. He was nervous, excitable, had no firm ground under his feet, and, above all, he had been unlucky. Even if he were guilty, anyway he deserved indulgence and the sympathy of all compassionate souls. He ought, of course, to be punished, but he was punished as it was by his conscience and the agonies he was enduring now while awaiting the sentence of his relations. The comparison with the army made by the Colonel was delightful, and did credit to his lofty intelligence; his appeal to their feeling of public duty spoke for the chivalry of his soul, but they must not forget that in each individual the citizen is closely linked with the Christian. . . .

"Shall we be false to civic duty," Ivan Markovitch exclaimed passionately, "if instead of punishing an erring boy we hold out to him a helping hand?"

Ivan Markovitch talked further of family honour. He had not the honour to belong to the Uskov family himself, but he knew their distinguished family went back to the thirteenth century; he did not forget for a minute, either, that his precious, beloved sister had been the wife of one of the representatives of that name. In short, the family was dear to him for many reasons, and he refused to admit the idea that, for the sake of a paltry fifteen hundred roubles, a blot should be cast on the escutcheon that was beyond all price. If all the motives he had brought forward were not sufficiently convincing, he, Ivan Markovitch, in conclusion, begged his listeners to ask themselves what was meant by crime? Crime is an immoral act founded upon ill-will. But is the will of man free? Philosophy has not yet given a positive answer to that question. Different views were held by the learned. The latest school of Lombroso, for instance, denies the freedom of the will, and considers every crime as the product of the purely anatomical peculiarities of the individual.

"Ivan Markovitch," said the Colonel, in a voice of entreaty, "we are talking seriously about an important matter, and you bring in Lombroso, you clever fellow. Think a little, what are you saying all this for? Can you imagine that all your thunderings and rhetoric will furnish an answer to the question?"

Sasha Uskov sat at the door and listened. He felt neither terror, shame, nor depression, but only weariness and inward emptiness. It seemed to him that it made absolutely no difference to him whether they forgave him or not; he had come here to hear his sentence and to explain himself simply because kind-hearted Ivan Markovitch had begged him to do so. He was not afraid of the future. It made no difference to him where he was: here in the hall, in prison, or in Siberia.

"If Siberia, then let it be Siberia, damn it all!"

He was sick of life and found it insufferably hard. He was inextricably involved in debt; he had not a farthing in his pocket; his family had become detestable to him; he would have to part from his friends and his women sooner or later, as they had begun to be too contemptuous of his sponging on them. The future looked black.

Sasha was indifferent, and was only disturbed by one circumstance; the other side of the door they were calling him a scoundrel and a criminal. Every minute he was on the point of jumping up, bursting into the study and shouting in answer to the detestable metallic voice of the Colonel:

"You are lying!"

"Criminal" is a dreadful word—that is what murderers, thieves, robbers are; in fact, wicked and morally hopeless people. And Sasha was very far from being all that. . . . It was true he owed a great deal and did not pay his debts. But debt is not a crime, and it is unusual for a man not to be in debt. The Colonel and Ivan Markovitch were both in debt. . . .

"What have I done wrong besides?" Sasha wondered.

He had discounted a forged note. But all the young men he knew did the same. Handrikov and Von Burst always forged IOU's from their parents or friends when their allowances were not paid at the regular time, and then when they got their money from home they redeemed them before they became due. Sasha had done the same, but had not redeemed the IOU because he had not got the money which Handrikov had promised to lend him. He was not to blame; it was the fault of circumstances. It was true that the use of another person's signature was considered reprehensible; but, still, it was not a crime but a generally accepted dodge, an ugly formality which injured no one and was quite harmless, for in forging the Colonel's signature Sasha had had no intention of causing anybody damage or loss.

"No, it doesn't mean that I am a criminal . . ." thought Sasha. "And it's not in my character to bring myself to commit a crime. I am soft, emotional. . . . When I have the money I help the poor. . . ."

Sasha was musing after this fashion while they went on talking the other side of the door.

"But, my friends, this is endless," the Colonel declared, getting excited. "Suppose we were to forgive him and pay the money. You know he would not give up leading a dissipated life, squandering money, making debts, going to our tailors and ordering suits in our names! Can you guarantee that this will be his last prank? As far as I am concerned, I have no faith whatever in his reforming!"

The official of the Treasury muttered something in reply; after him Ivan Markovitch began talking blandly and suavely again. The Colonel moved his chair impatiently and drowned the other's words with his detestable metallic voice. At last the door opened and Ivan Markovitch came out of the study; there were patches of red on his lean shaven face.

"Come along," he said, taking Sasha by the hand. "Come and speak frankly from your heart. Without pride, my dear boy, humbly and from your heart."

Sasha went into the study. The official of the Treasury was sitting down; the Colonel was standing before the table with one hand in his pocket and one knee on a chair. It was smoky and stifling in the study. Sasha did not look at the official or the Colonel; he felt suddenly ashamed and uncomfortable. He looked uneasily at Ivan Markovitch and muttered:

"I'll pay it . . . I'll give it back. . . ."

"What did you expect when you discounted the IOU?" he heard a metallic voice.

"I . . . Handrikov promised to lend me the money before now."

Sasha could say no more. He went out of the study and sat down again on the chair near the door.

He would have been glad to go away altogether at once, but he was choking with hatred and he awfully wanted to remain, to tear the Colonel to pieces, to say something rude to him. He sat trying to think of something violent and effective to say to his hated uncle, and at that moment a woman's figure, shrouded in the twilight, appeared at the drawing-room door. It was the Colonel's wife. She beckoned Sasha to her, and, wringing her hands, said, weeping:

"Alexandre, I know you don't like me, but . . . listen to me; listen, I beg you. . . . But, my dear, how can this have happened? Why, it's awful, awful! For goodness' sake, beg them, defend yourself, entreat them."

Sasha looked at her quivering shoulders, at the big tears that were rolling down her cheeks, heard behind his back the hollow, nervous voices of worried and exhausted people, and shrugged his shoulders. He had not in the least expected that his aristocratic relations would raise such a tempest over a paltry fifteen hundred roubles! He could not understand her tears nor the quiver of their voices.

An hour later he heard that the Colonel was getting the best of it; the uncles were finally inclining to let the case go for trial.

"The matter's settled," said the Colonel, sighing. "Enough."

After this decision all the uncles, even the emphatic Colonel, became noticeably depressed. A silence followed.

"Merciful Heavens!" sighed Ivan Markovitch. "My poor sister!"

And he began saying in a subdued voice that most likely his sister, Sasha's mother, was present unseen in the study at that moment. He felt in his soul how the unhappy, saintly woman was weeping, grieving, and begging for her boy. For the sake of her peace beyond the grave, they ought to spare Sasha.

The sound of a muffled sob was heard. Ivan Markovitch was weeping and muttering something which it was impossible to catch through the door. The Colonel got up and paced from corner to corner. The long conversation began over again.

But then the clock in the drawing-room struck two. The family council was over. To avoid seeing the person who had moved him to such wrath, the Colonel went from the study, not into the hall, but into the vestibule. . . . Ivan Markovitch came out into the hall. . . . He was agitated and rubbing his hands joyfully. His tear-stained eyes looked good-humoured and his mouth was twisted into a smile.

"Capital," he said to Sasha. "Thank God! You can go home, my dear, and sleep tranquilly. We have decided to pay the sum, but on condition that you repent and come with me tomorrow into the country and set to work."

A minute later Ivan Markovitch and Sasha in their great-coats and caps were going down the stairs. The uncle was muttering something edifying. Sasha did not listen, but felt as though some uneasy weight were gradually slipping off his shoulders. They had forgiven him; he was free! A gust of joy sprang up within him and sent a sweet chill to his heart. He longed to breathe, to move swiftly, to live! Glancing at the street lamps and the black sky, he remembered that Von Burst was celebrating his name-day that evening at the "Bear," and again a rush of joy flooded his soul. . . .

"I am going!" he decided.

But then he remembered he had not a farthing, that the companions he was going to would despise him at once for his empty pockets. He must get hold of some money, come what may!

"Uncle, lend me a hundred roubles," he said to Ivan Markovitch.

His uncle, surprised, looked into his face and backed against a lamp-post.

"Give it to me," said Sasha, shifting impatiently from one foot to the other and beginning to pant. "Uncle, I entreat you, give me a hundred roubles."

His face worked; he trembled, and seemed on the point of attacking his uncle. . . .

"Won't you?" he kept asking, seeing that his uncle was still amazed and did not understand. "Listen. If you don't, I'll give myself up tomorrow! I won't let you pay the IOU! I'll present another false note tomorrow!"

Petrified, muttering something incoherent in his horror, Ivan

Markovitch took a hundred-rouble note out of his pocket-book and gave it to Sasha. The young man took it and walked rapidly away from him. . . .

Taking a sledge, Sasha grew calmer, and felt a rush of joy within him again. The "rights of youth" of which kind-hearted Ivan Markovitch had spoken at the family council woke up and asserted themselves. Sasha pictured the drinking-party before him, and, among the bottles, the women, and his friends, the thought flashed through his mind:

"Now I see that I am a criminal; yes, I am a criminal."

NOTES

Lombroso: Ceasare Lombroso (1836-1909) was an Italian criminologist who suggested that criminals can be identified by certain physical characteristics

name-day: Russians celebrate the feast day of the saint after whom they are named

THE KISS

At eight o'clock on the evening of the twentieth of May all the six batteries of the N—— Reserve Artillery Brigade halted for the night in the village of Myestetchki on their way to camp. When the general commotion was at its height, while some officers were busily occupied around the guns, while others, gathered together in the square near the church enclosure, were listening to the quartermasters, a man in civilian dress, riding a strange horse, came into sight round the church. The little dun-coloured horse with a good neck and a short tail came, moving not straight forward, but as it were sideways, with a sort of dance step, as though it were being lashed about the legs. When he reached the officers the man on the horse took off his hat and said:

"His Excellency Lieutenant-General von Rabbek invites the gentlemen to drink tea with him this minute. . . ."

The horse turned, danced, and retired sideways; the messenger raised his hat once more, and in an instant disappeared with his strange horse behind the church.

"What the devil does it mean?" grumbled some of the officers, dispersing to their quarters. "One is sleepy, and here this Von Rabbek with his tea! We know what tea means."

The officers of all the six batteries remembered vividly an incident of the previous year, when during manoeuvres they, together with the officers of a Cossack regiment, were in the same way invited to tea by a count who had an estate in the neighbourhood and was a retired army officer: the hospitable and genial count made much of them, fed them, and gave them drink, refused to let them go to their quarters in the village and made them stay the night. All that, of course, was very nice—nothing better could be desired, but the worst of it was, the old army officer was so carried away by the pleasure of the young men's company that till sunrise he was telling the officers anecdotes of his glorious past, taking them over the house, showing them expensive pictures, old engravings, rare guns, reading them autograph letters from great people, while the weary and exhausted officers looked and listened, longing for their beds and yawning in their sleeves; when at last their host let them go, it was too late for sleep.

Might not this Von Rabbek be just such another? Whether he were or not, there was no help for it. The officers changed their uniforms, brushed themselves, and went all together in search of the gentleman's house. In the square by the church they were told they could get to His Excellency's by the lower path—going down behind the church to the river, going along the bank to the garden, and there an avenue would taken them to the house; or by the upper way—straight from the church by the road which, half a mile from the village, led right up to His Excellency's granaries. The officers decided to go by the upper way.

"What Von Rabbek is it?" they wondered on the way. "Surely not the one who was in command of the N—— cavalry division at Plevna?"

"No, that was not Von Rabbek, but simply Rabbe and no 'von.'"

"What lovely weather!"

At the first of the granaries the road divided in two: one branch went straight on and vanished in the evening darkness, the other led to the owner's house on the right. The officers turned to the right and began to speak more softly. . . . On both sides of the road stretched stone granaries with red roofs, heavy and sullen-looking, very much like barracks of a district town. Ahead of them gleamed the windows of the manor-house.

"A good omen, gentlemen," said one of the officers. "Our setter is the foremost of all; no doubt he scents game ahead of us! . . ."

Lieutenant Lobytko, who was walking in front, a tall and stalwart fellow, though entirely without moustache (he was over five-and-twenty, yet for some reason there was no sign of hair on his round, well-fed face), renowned in the brigade for his peculiar faculty for divining the presence of women at a distance, turned round and said:

"Yes, there must be women here; I feel that by instinct."

On the threshold the officers were met by Von Rabbek himself, a comely-looking man of sixty in civilian dress. Shaking hands with his guests, he said that he was very glad and happy to see them, but begged them earnestly for God's sake to excuse him for not asking them to stay the night; two sisters with their children, some brothers, and some neighbours, had come on a visit to him, so that he had not one spare room left.

The General shook hands with every one, made his apologies, and smiled, but it was evident by his face that he was by no means so delighted as their last year's count, and that he had invited the officers simply because, in his opinion, it was a social obligation to do so. And the officers themselves, as they walked up the softly carpeted stairs, as they listened to him, felt that they had been invited to this house simply because it would have been awkward not to invite them; and at the sight of the footmen, who hastened to light the lamps in the entrance below and in the anteroom above, they began to feel as though they had brought uneasiness and discomfort into the house with them. In a house in which two sisters and their children, brothers, and neighbours were gathered together, probably on account of some family festivity, or event, how could the presence of nineteen unknown officers possibly be welcome?

At the entrance to the drawing-room the officers were met by a tall, graceful old lady with black eyebrows and a long face, very much like the Empress Eugénie. Smiling graciously and majestically, she said she was glad and happy to see her guests, and apologized that her husband and she were on this occasion unable to invite messieurs les officiers to stay the night. From her beautiful majestic smile, which instantly vanished from her face every time she turned away from her guests, it was evident that she had seen numbers of officers in her day, that she was in no humour for them now, and if she invited them to her house and apologized for not doing more, it was only because her breeding and position in society required it of her.

When the officers went into the big dining-room, there were about a dozen people, men and ladies, young and old, sitting at tea at the end of a long table. A group of men was dimly visible behind their chairs, wrapped in a haze of cigar smoke; and in the midst of them stood a lanky young man with red whiskers, talking loudly, with a lisp, in English. Through a door beyond the group could be seen a light room with pale blue furniture.

"Gentlemen, there are so many of you that it is impossible to introduce you all!" said the General in a loud voice, trying to sound very cheerful. "Make each other's acquaintance, gentlemen, without any ceremony!"

The officers—some with very serious and even stern faces, others with forced smiles, and all feeling extremely awkward—somehow made their bows and sat down to tea.

The most ill at ease of them all was Ryabovitch—a little officer in spectacles, with sloping shoulders, and whiskers like a lynx's. While some of his comrades assumed a serious expression, while others wore forced smiles, his face, his lynx-like whiskers, and spectacles seemed to say: "I am the shyest, most modest, and most undistinguished officer in the whole brigade!" At first, on going into the room and sitting down to the table, he could not fix his attention on any one face or object. The faces, the dresses, the cut-glass decanters of brandy, the steam from the glasses, the moulded cornices—all blended in one general impression that inspired in Ryabovitch alarm and a desire to hide his head. Like a lecturer making his first appearance before the public, he saw everything that was before his eyes, but apparently only had a dim understanding of it (among physiologists this condition, when the subject sees but does not understand, is called psychical blindness). After a little while, growing accustomed to his surroundings, Ryabovitch saw clearly and began to observe. As a shy man, unused to society, what struck him first was that in which he had always been deficient—namely, the extraordinary boldness of his new acquaintances. Von Rabbek, his wife, two elderly ladies, a young lady in a lilac dress, and the young man with the red whiskers, who was, it appeared, a younger son of Von Rabbek, very cleverly, as though they had rehearsed it beforehand, took seats between the officers, and at once got up a heated discussion in which the visitors could not help taking part. The lilac young lady hotly asserted that the artillery had a much better time than the cavalry and the infantry, while Von Rabbek and the elderly ladies maintained the opposite. A brisk interchange of talk followed. Ryabovitch watched the lilac young lady who argued so hotly about what was unfamiliar and utterly uninteresting to her, and watched artificial smiles come and go on her face.

Von Rabbek and his family skilfully drew the officers into the discussion, and meanwhile kept a sharp lookout over their glasses and mouths, to see whether all of them were drinking, whether all had enough sugar, why some one was not eating cakes or not drinking brandy. And the longer Ryabovitch watched and listened, the more he was attracted by this insincere but splendidly disciplined family.

After tea the officers went into the drawing-room. Lieutenant Lobytko's instinct had not deceived him. There were a great number of girls and young married ladies. The "setter" lieutenant was soon standing by a very young, fair girl in a black dress, and, bending down to her jauntily, as though leaning on an unseen sword, smiled and shrugged his shoulders coquettishly. He probably talked very interesting nonsense, for the fair girl looked at his well-fed face condescendingly and asked indifferently, "Really?" And from that uninterested "Really?" the setter, had he been intelligent, might have concluded that she would never call him to heel.

The piano struck up; the melancholy strains of a valse floated out of the wide open windows, and every one, for some reason, remembered that it was spring, a May evening. Every one was conscious of the fragrance of roses, of lilac, and of the young leaves of the poplar. Ryabovitch, in whom the brandy he had drunk made itself felt, under the influence of the music stole a glance towards the window, smiled, and began watching the movements of the women, and it seemed to him that the smell of roses, of poplars, and lilac came not from the garden, but from the ladies' faces and dresses.

Von Rabbek's son invited a scraggy-looking young lady to dance, and waltzed round the room twice with her. Lobytko, gliding over the parquet floor, flew up to the lilac young lady and whirled her away. Dancing began. . . . Ryabovitch stood near the door among those who were not dancing and looked on. He had never once danced in his whole life, and he had never once in his life put his arm round the waist of a respectable woman. He was highly delighted that a man should in the sight of all take a girl he did not know round the waist and offer her his shoulder to put her hand on, but he could not imagine himself in the position of such a man. There were times when he envied the boldness and swagger of his companions and was inwardly wretched; the consciousness that he was timid, that he was round-shouldered and uninteresting, that he had a long waist and lynx-like whiskers, had deeply mortified him, but with years he had grown used to this feeling, and now, looking at his comrades dancing or loudly talking, he no longer envied them, but only felt touched and mournful.

When the quadrille began, young Von Rabbek came up to those who were not dancing and invited two officers to have a game at billiards. The officers accepted and went with him out of the drawing-room. Ryabovitch, having nothing to do and wishing to take part in the general movement, slouched after them. From the big drawing-room they went into the little drawing-room, then into a narrow corridor with a glass roof, and thence into a room in which on their entrance three sleepy-looking footmen jumped up quickly from the sofa. At last, after passing through a long succession of rooms, young Von Rabbek and the officers came into a small room where there was a billiard-table. They began to play.

Ryabovitch, who had never played any game but cards, stood near the billiard-table and looked indifferently at the players, while they in unbuttoned coats, with cues in their hands, stepped about, made puns, and kept shouting out unintelligible words.

The players took no notice of him, and only now and then one of them, shoving him with his elbow or accidentally touching him with the end of his cue, would turn round and say "Pardon!" Before the first game was over he was weary of it, and began to feel he was not wanted and in the way. . . . He felt disposed to return to the drawing-room, and he went out.

On his way back he met with a little adventure. When he had gone half-way he noticed he had taken a wrong turning. He distinctly remembered that he ought to meet three sleepy footmen on his way, but he had passed five or six rooms, and those sleepy figures seemed to have vanished into the earth. Noticing his mistake, he walked back a little way and turned to the right; he found himself in a little dark room which he had not seen on his way to the billiard-room. After standing there a little while, he resolutely opened the first door that met his eyes and walked into an absolutely dark room. Straight in front could be seen the crack in the doorway through which there was a gleam of vivid light; from the other side of the door came the muffled sound of a melancholy mazurka. Here, too, as in the drawing-room, the windows were wide open and there was a smell of poplars, lilac and roses. . . .

Ryabovitch stood still in hesitation. . . . At that moment, to his surprise, he heard hurried footsteps and the rustling of a dress, a breathless feminine voice whispered "At last!" And two soft, fragrant, unmistakably feminine arms were clasped about his neck; a warm cheek was pressed to his cheek, and simultaneously there was the sound of a kiss. But at once the bestower of the kiss uttered a faint shriek and skipped back from him, as it seemed to Ryabovitch, with aversion. He, too, almost shrieked and rushed towards the gleam of light at the door. . . .

When he went back into the drawing-room his heart was beating and his hands were trembling so noticeably that he made haste to hide them behind his back. At first he was tormented by shame and dread that the whole drawing-room knew that he had just been kissed and embraced by a woman. He shrank into himself and looked uneasily about him, but as he became convinced that people were dancing and talking as calmly as ever, he gave himself up entirely to the new sensation which he had never experienced before in his life. Something strange was happening to him. . . . His neck, round which soft, fragrant arms had so lately been clasped, seemed to him to be anointed with oil; on his left cheek near his moustache where the unknown had kissed him there was a faint chilly tingling sensation as from peppermint drops, and the more he rubbed the place the more distinct was the chilly sensation; all over, from head to foot, he was full of a strange new feeling which grew stronger and stronger . . . . He wanted to dance, to talk, to run into the garden, to laugh aloud. . . . He quite forgot that he was round-shouldered and uninteresting, that he had lynx-like whiskers and an "undistinguished appearance" (that was how his appearance had been described by some ladies whose conversation he had accidentally overheard). When Von Rabbek's wife happened to pass by him, he gave her such a broad and friendly smile that she stood still and looked at him inquiringly.

"I like your house immensely!" he said, setting his spectacles straight.

The General's wife smiled and said that the house had belonged to her father; then she asked whether his parents were living, whether he had long been in the army, why he was so thin, and so on. . . . After receiving answers to her questions, she went on, and after his conversation with her his smiles were more friendly than ever, and he thought he was surrounded by splendid people. . . .

At supper Ryabovitch ate mechanically everything offered him, drank, and without listening to anything, tried to understand what had just happened to him. . . . The adventure was of a mysterious and romantic character, but it was not difficult to explain it. No doubt some girl or young married lady had arranged a tryst with some one in the dark room; had waited a long time, and being nervous and excited had taken Ryabovitch for her hero; this was the more probable as Ryabovitch had stood still hesitating in the dark room, so that he, too, had seemed like a person expecting something. . . . This was how Ryabovitch explained to himself the kiss he had received.

"And who is she?" he wondered, looking round at the women's faces. "She must be young, for elderly ladies don't give rendezvous. That she was a lady, one could tell by the rustle of her dress, her perfume, her voice. . . ."

His eyes rested on the lilac young lady, and he thought her very attractive; she had beautiful shoulders and arms, a clever face, and a delightful voice. Ryabovitch, looking at her, hoped that she and no one else was his unknown. . . . But she laughed somehow artificially and wrinkled up her long nose, which seemed to him to make her look old. Then he turned his eyes upon the fair girl in a black dress. She was younger, simpler, and more genuine, had a charming brow, and drank very daintily out of her wineglass. Ryabovitch now hoped that it was she. But soon he began to think her face flat, and fixed his eyes upon the one next her.

"It's difficult to guess," he thought, musing. "If one takes the shoulders and arms of the lilac one only, adds the brow of the fair one and the eyes of the one on the left of Lobytko, then . . ."

He made a combination of these things in his mind and so formed the image of the girl who had kissed him, the image that he wanted her to have, but could not find at the table. . . .

After supper, replete and exhilarated, the officers began to take leave and say thank you. Von Rabbek and his wife began again apologizing that they could not ask them to stay the night.

"Very, very glad to have met you, gentlemen," said Von Rabbek, and this time sincerely (probably because people are far more sincere and good-humoured at speeding their parting guests than on meeting them). "Delighted. I hope you will come on your way back! Don't stand on ceremony! Where are you going? Do you want to go by the upper way? No, go across the garden; it's nearer here by the lower way."

The officers went out into the garden. After the bright light and the noise the garden seemed very dark and quiet. They walked in silence all the way to the gate. They were a little drunk, pleased, and in good spirits, but the darkness and silence made them thoughtful for a minute. Probably the same idea occurred to each one of them as to Ryabovitch: would there ever come a time for them when, like Von Rabbek, they would have a large house, a family, a garden— when they, too, would be able to welcome people, even though insincerely, feed them, make them drunk and contented?

Going out of the garden gate, they all began talking at once and laughing loudly about nothing. They were walking now along the little path that led down to the river, and then ran along the water's edge, winding round the bushes on the bank, the pools, and the willows that overhung the water. The bank and the path were scarcely visible, and the other bank was entirely plunged in darkness. Stars were reflected here and there on the dark water; they quivered and were broken up on the surface—and from that alone it could be seen that the river was flowing rapidly. It was still. Drowsy curlews cried plaintively on the further bank, and in one of the bushes on the nearest side a nightingale was trilling loudly, taking no notice of the crowd of officers. The officers stood round the bush, touched it, but the nightingale went on singing.

"What a fellow!" they exclaimed approvingly. "We stand beside him and he takes not a bit of notice! What a rascal!"

At the end of the way the path went uphill, and, skirting the church enclosure, turned into the road. Here the officers, tired with walking uphill, sat down and lighted their cigarettes. On the other side of the river a murky red fire came into sight, and having nothing better to do, they spent a long time in discussing whether it was a camp fire or a light in a window, or something else. . . . Ryabovitch, too, looked at the light, and he fancied that the light looked and winked at him, as though it knew about the kiss.

On reaching his quarters, Ryabovitch undressed as quickly as possible and got into bed. Lobytko and Lieutenant Merzlyakov—a peaceable, silent fellow, who was considered in his own circle a highly educated officer, and was always, whenever it was possible, reading the "Vyestnik Evropi," which he carried about with him everywhere— were quartered in the same hut with Ryabovitch. Lobytko undressed, walked up and down the room for a long while with the air of a man who has not been satisfied, and sent his orderly for beer. Merzlyakov got into bed, put a candle by his pillow and plunged into reading the "Vyestnik Evropi."

"Who was she?" Ryabovitch wondered, looking at the smoky ceiling.

His neck still felt as though he had been anointed with oil, and there was still the chilly sensation near his mouth as though from peppermint drops. The shoulders and arms of the young lady in lilac, the brow and the truthful eyes of the fair girl in black, waists, dresses, and brooches, floated through his imagination. He tried to fix his attention on these images, but they danced about, broke up and flickered. When these images vanished altogether from the broad dark background which every man sees when he closes his eyes, he began to hear hurried footsteps, the rustle of skirts, the sound of a kiss and—an intense groundless joy took possession of him . . . . Abandoning himself to this joy, he heard the orderly return and announce that there was no beer. Lobytko was terribly indignant, and began pacing up and down again.

"Well, isn't he an idiot?" he kept saying, stopping first before Ryabovitch and then before Merzlyakov. "What a fool and a dummy a man must be not to get hold of any beer! Eh? Isn't he a scoundrel?"

"Of course you can't get beer here," said Merzlyakov, not removing his eyes from the "Vyestnik Evropi."

"Oh! Is that your opinion?" Lobytko persisted. "Lord have mercy upon us, if you dropped me on the moon I'd find you beer and women directly! I'll go and find some at once. . . . You may call me an impostor if I don't!"

He spent a long time in dressing and pulling on his high boots, then finished smoking his cigarette in silence and went out.

"Rabbek, Grabbek, Labbek," he muttered, stopping in the outer room. "I don't care to go alone, damn it all! Ryabovitch, wouldn't you like to go for a walk? Eh?"

Receiving no answer, he returned, slowly undressed and got into bed. Merzlyakov sighed, put the "Vyestnik Evropi" away, and put out the light.

"H'm! . . ." muttered Lobytko, lighting a cigarette in the dark.

Ryabovitch pulled the bed-clothes over his head, curled himself up in bed, and tried to gather together the floating images in his mind and to combine them into one whole. But nothing came of it. He soon fell asleep, and his last thought was that some one had caressed him and made him happy—that something extraordinary, foolish, but joyful and delightful, had come into his life. The thought did not leave him even in his sleep.

When he woke up the sensations of oil on his neck and the chill of peppermint about his lips had gone, but joy flooded his heart just as the day before. He looked enthusiastically at the window-frames, gilded by the light of the rising sun, and listened to the movement of the passers-by in the street. People were talking loudly close to the window. Lebedetsky, the commander of Ryabovitch's battery, who had only just overtaken the brigade, was talking to his sergeant at the top of his voice, being always accustomed to shout.

"What else?" shouted the commander.

"When they were shoeing yesterday, your high nobility, they drove a nail into Pigeon's hoof. The vet. put on clay and vinegar; they are leading him apart now. And also, your honour, Artemyev got drunk yesterday, and the lieutenant ordered him to be put in the limber of a spare gun-carriage."

The sergeant reported that Karpov had forgotten the new cords for the trumpets and the rings for the tents, and that their honours, the officers, had spent the previous evening visiting General Von Rabbek. In the middle of this conversation the red-bearded face of Lebedetsky appeared in the window. He screwed up his short-sighted eyes, looking at the sleepy faces of the officers, and said good-morning to them.

"Is everything all right?" he asked.

"One of the horses has a sore neck from the new collar," answered Lobytko, yawning.

The commander sighed, thought a moment, and said in a loud voice:

"I am thinking of going to see Alexandra Yevgrafovna. I must call on her. Well, good-bye. I shall catch you up in the evening."

A quarter of an hour later the brigade set off on its way. When it was moving along the road by the granaries, Ryabovitch looked at the house on the right. The blinds were down in all the windows. Evidently the household was still asleep. The one who had kissed Ryabovitch the day before was asleep, too. He tried to imagine her asleep. The wide-open windows of the bedroom, the green branches peeping in, the morning freshness, the scent of the poplars, lilac, and roses, the bed, a chair, and on it the skirts that had rustled the day before, the little slippers, the little watch on the table —all this he pictured to himself clearly and distinctly, but the features of the face, the sweet sleepy smile, just what was characteristic and important, slipped through his imagination like quicksilver through the fingers. When he had ridden on half a mile, he looked back: the yellow church, the house, and the river, were all bathed in light; the river with its bright green banks, with the blue sky reflected in it and glints of silver in the sunshine here and there, was very beautiful. Ryabovitch gazed for the last time at Myestetchki, and he felt as sad as though he were parting with something very near and dear to him.

And before him on the road lay nothing but long familiar, uninteresting pictures. . . . To right and to left, fields of young rye and buckwheat with rooks hopping about in them. If one looked ahead, one saw dust and the backs of men's heads; if one looked back, one saw the same dust and faces. . . . Foremost of all marched four men with sabres—this was the vanguard. Next, behind, the crowd of singers, and behind them the trumpeters on horseback. The vanguard and the chorus of singers, like torch-bearers in a funeral procession, often forgot to keep the regulation distance and pushed a long way ahead. . . . Ryabovitch was with the first cannon of the fifth battery. He could see all the four batteries moving in front of him. For any one not a military man this long tedious procession of a moving brigade seems an intricate and unintelligible muddle; one cannot understand why there are so many people round one cannon, and why it is drawn by so many horses in such a strange network of harness, as though it really were so terrible and heavy. To Ryabovitch it was all perfectly comprehensible and therefore uninteresting. He had known for ever so long why at the head of each battery there rode a stalwart bombardier, and why he was called a bombardier; immediately behind this bombardier could be seen the horsemen of the first and then of the middle units. Ryabovitch knew that the horses on which they rode, those on the left, were called one name, while those on the right were called another—it was extremely uninteresting. Behind the horsemen came two shaft-horses. On one of them sat a rider with the dust of yesterday on his back and a clumsy and funny-looking piece of wood on his leg. Ryabovitch knew the object of this piece of wood, and did not think it funny. All the riders waved their whips mechanically and shouted from time to time. The cannon itself was ugly. On the fore part lay sacks of oats covered with canvas, and the cannon itself was hung all over with kettles, soldiers' knapsacks, bags, and looked like some small harmless animal surrounded for some unknown reason by men and horses. To the leeward of it marched six men, the gunners, swinging their arms. After the cannon there came again more bombardiers, riders, shaft-horses, and behind them another cannon, as ugly and unimpressive as the first. After the second followed a third, a fourth; near the fourth an officer, and so on. There were six batteries in all in the brigade, and four cannons in each battery. The procession covered half a mile; it ended in a string of wagons near which an extremely attractive creature—the ass, Magar, brought by a battery commander from Turkey—paced pensively with his long-eared head drooping.

Ryabovitch looked indifferently before and behind, at the backs of heads and at faces; at any other time he would have been half asleep, but now he was entirely absorbed in his new agreeable thoughts. At first when the brigade was setting off on the march he tried to persuade himself that the incident of the kiss could only be interesting as a mysterious little adventure, that it was in reality trivial, and to think of it seriously, to say the least of it, was stupid; but now he bade farewell to logic and gave himself up to dreams. . . . At one moment he imagined himself in Von Rabbek's drawing-room beside a girl who was like the young lady in lilac and the fair girl in black; then he would close his eyes and see himself with another, entirely unknown girl, whose features were very vague. In his imagination he talked, caressed her, leaned on her shoulder, pictured war, separation, then meeting again, supper with his wife, children. . . .

"Brakes on!" the word of command rang out every time they went downhill.

He, too, shouted "Brakes on!" and was afraid this shout would disturb his reverie and bring him back to reality. . . .

As they passed by some landowner's estate Ryabovitch looked over the fence into the garden. A long avenue, straight as a ruler, strewn with yellow sand and bordered with young birch-trees, met his eyes. . . . With the eagerness of a man given up to dreaming, he pictured to himself little feminine feet tripping along yellow sand, and quite unexpectedly had a clear vision in his imagination of the girl who had kissed him and whom he had succeeded in picturing to himself the evening before at supper. This image remained in his brain and did not desert him again.

At midday there was a shout in the rear near the string of wagons:

"Easy! Eyes to the left! Officers!"

The general of the brigade drove by in a carriage with a pair of white horses. He stopped near the second battery, and shouted something which no one understood. Several officers, among them Ryabovitch, galloped up to them.

"Well?" asked the general, blinking his red eyes. "Are there any sick?"

Receiving an answer, the general, a little skinny man, chewed, thought for a moment and said, addressing one of the officers:

"One of your drivers of the third cannon has taken off his leg-guard and hung it on the fore part of the cannon, the rascal. Reprimand him."

He raised his eyes to Ryabovitch and went on:

"It seems to me your front strap is too long."

Making a few other tedious remarks, the general looked at Lobytko and grinned.

"You look very melancholy today, Lieutenant Lobytko," he said. "Are you pining for Madame Lopuhov? Eh? Gentlemen, he is pining for Madame Lopuhov."

The lady in question was a very stout and tall person who had long passed her fortieth year. The general, who had a predilection for solid ladies, whatever their ages, suspected a similar taste in his officers. The officers smiled respectfully. The general, delighted at having said something very amusing and biting, laughed loudly, touched his coachman's back, and saluted. The carriage rolled on. . . .

"All I am dreaming about now which seems to me so impossible and unearthly is really quite an ordinary thing," thought Ryabovitch, looking at the clouds of dust racing after the general's carriage. "It's all very ordinary, and every one goes through it. . . . That general, for instance, has once been in love; now he is married and has children. Captain Vahter, too, is married and beloved, though the nape of his neck is very red and ugly and he has no waist. . . . Salrnanov is coarse and very Tatar, but he has had a love affair that has ended in marriage. . . . I am the same as every one else, and I, too, shall have the same experience as every one else, sooner or later. . . ."

And the thought that he was an ordinary person, and that his life was ordinary, delighted him and gave him courage. He pictured her and his happiness as he pleased, and put no rein on his imagination.

When the brigade reached their halting-place in the evening, and the officers were resting in their tents, Ryabovitch, Merzlyakov, and Lobytko were sitting round a box having supper. Merzlyakov ate without haste, and, as he munched deliberately, read the "Vyestnik Evropi," which he held on his knees. Lobytko talked incessantly and kept filling up his glass with beer, and Ryabovitch, whose head was confused from dreaming all day long, drank and said nothing. After three glasses he got a little drunk, felt weak, and had an irresistible desire to impart his new sensations to his comrades.

"A strange thing happened to me at those Von Rabbeks'," he began, trying to put an indifferent and ironical tone into his voice. "You know I went into the billiard-room. . . ."

He began describing very minutely the incident of the kiss, and a moment later relapsed into silence. . . . In the course of that moment he had told everything, and it surprised him dreadfully to find how short a time it took him to tell it. He had imagined that he could have been telling the story of the kiss till next morning. Listening to him, Lobytko, who was a great liar and consequently believed no one, looked at him sceptically and laughed. Merzlyakov twitched his eyebrows and, without removing his eyes from the "Vyestnik Evropi," said:

"That's an odd thing! How strange! . . . throws herself on a man's neck, without addressing him by name. .. . She must be some sort of hysterical neurotic."

"Yes, she must," Ryabovitch agreed.

"A similar thing once happened to me," said Lobytko, assuming a scared expression. "I was going last year to Kovno. . . . I took a second-class ticket. The train was crammed, and it was impossible to sleep. I gave the guard half a rouble; he took my luggage and led me to another compartment. . . . I lay down and covered myself with a rug. . . . It was dark, you understand. Suddenly I felt some one touch me on the shoulder and breathe in my face. I made a movement with my hand and felt somebody's elbow. . . . I opened my eyes and only imagine—a woman. Black eyes, lips red as a prime salmon, nostrils breathing passionately—a bosom like a buffer. . . ."

"Excuse me," Merzlyakov interrupted calmly, "I understand about the bosom, but how could you see the lips if it was dark?"

Lobytko began trying to put himself right and laughing at Merzlyakov's unimaginativeness. It made Ryabovitch wince. He walked away from the box, got into bed, and vowed never to confide again.

Camp life began. . . . The days flowed by, one very much like another. All those days Ryabovitch felt, thought, and behaved as though he were in love. Every morning when his orderly handed him water to wash with, and he sluiced his head with cold water, he thought there was something warm and delightful in his life.

In the evenings when his comrades began talking of love and women, he would listen, and draw up closer; and he wore the expression of a soldier when he hears the description of a battle in which he has taken part. And on the evenings when the officers, out on the spree with the setter—Lobytko—at their head, made Don Juan excursions to the "suburb," and Ryabovitch took part in such excursions, he always was sad, felt profoundly guilty, and inwardly begged her forgiveness. . . . In hours of leisure or on sleepless nights, when he felt moved to recall his childhood, his father and mother— everything near and dear, in fact, he invariably thought of Myestetchki, the strange horse, Von Rabbek, his wife who was like the Empress Eugénie, the dark room, the crack of light at the door. . . .

On the thirty-first of August he went back from the camp, not with the whole brigade, but with only two batteries of it. He was dreaming and excited all the way, as though he were going back to his native place. He had an intense longing to see again the strange horse, the church, the insincere family of the Von Rabbeks, the dark room. The "inner voice," which so often deceives lovers, whispered to him for some reason that he would be sure to see her . . . and he was tortured by the questions, How he should meet her? What he would talk to her about? Whether she had forgotten the kiss? If the worst came to the worst, he thought, even if he did not meet her, it would be a pleasure to him merely to go through the dark room and recall the past. . . .

Towards evening there appeared on the horizon the familiar church and white granaries. Ryabovitch's heart beat. . . . He did not hear the officer who was riding beside him and saying something to him, he forgot everything, and looked eagerly at the river shining in the distance, at the roof of the house, at the dovecote round which the pigeons were circling in the light of the setting sun.

When they reached the church and were listening to the billeting orders, he expected every second that a man on horseback would come round the church enclosure and invite the officers to tea, but . . . the billeting orders were read, the officers were in haste to go on to the village, and the man on horseback did not appear.

"Von Rabbek will hear at once from the peasants that we have come and will send for us," thought Ryabovitch, as he went into the hut, unable to understand why a comrade was lighting a candle and why the orderlies were hurriedly setting samovars. . . .

A painful uneasiness took possession of him. He lay down, then got up and looked out of the window to see whether the messenger were coming. But there was no sign of him.

He lay down again, but half an hour later he got up, and, unable to restrain his uneasiness, went into the street and strode towards the church. It was dark and deserted in the square near the church . . . . Three soldiers were standing silent in a row where the road began to go downhill. Seeing Ryabovitch, they roused themselves and saluted. He returned the salute and began to go down the familiar path.

On the further side of the river the whole sky was flooded with crimson: the moon was rising; two peasant women, talking loudly, were picking cabbage in the kitchen garden; behind the kitchen garden there were some dark huts. . . . And everything on the near side of the river was just as it had been in May: the path, the bushes, the willows overhanging the water . . . but there was no sound of the brave nightingale, and no scent of poplar and fresh grass.

Reaching the garden, Ryabovitch looked in at the gate. The

garden was dark and still. . . . He could see nothing but the white stems of the nearest birch-trees and a little bit of the avenue; all the rest melted together into a dark blur. Ryabovitch looked and listened eagerly, but after waiting for a quarter of an hour without hearing a sound or catching a glimpse of a light, he trudged back. . . .

He went down to the river. The General's bath-house and the bath-sheets on the rail of the little bridge showed white before him. . . . He went on to the bridge, stood a little, and, quite unnecessarily, touched the sheets. They felt rough and cold. He looked down at the water. . . . The river ran rapidly and with a faintly audible gurgle round the piles of the bath-house. The red moon was reflected near the left bank; little ripples ran over the reflection, stretching it out, breaking it into bits, and seemed trying to carry it away.

"How stupid, how stupid!" thought Ryabovitch, looking at the running water. "How unintelligent it all is!"

Now that he expected nothing, the incident of the kiss, his impatience, his vague hopes and disappointment, presented themselves in a clear light. It no longer seemed to him strange that he had not seen the General's messenger, and that he would never see the girl who had accidentally kissed him instead of some one else; on the contrary, it would have been strange if he had seen her. . . .

The water was running, he knew not where or why, just as it did in May. In May it had flowed into the great river, from the great river into the sea; then it had risen in vapour, turned into rain, and perhaps the very same water was running now before Ryabovitch's eyes again. . . . What for? Why?

And the whole world, the whole of life, seemed to Ryabovitch an unintelligible, aimless jest. . . . And turning his eyes from the water and looking at the sky, he remembered again how fate in the person of an unknown woman had by chance caressed him, he remembered his summer dreams and fancies, and his life struck him as extraordinarily meagre, poverty-stricken, and colourless. . . .

When he went back to his hut he did not find one of his comrades. The orderly informed him that they had all gone to "General von Rabbek's, who had sent a messenger on horseback to invite them. . . ."

For an instant there was a flash of joy in Ryabovitch's heart, but he quenched it at once, got into bed, and in his wrath with his fate, as though to spite it, did not go to the General's.

NOTES

Empress Eugénie: consort of Napoleon III and Empress of France from 1853-1870

"Vyestnik Evropi": Messenger of Europe

vet.: Chekhov actually used the word "feldscher," doctor's assistant

rings for the tents: tent-stakes

Tatar: a member of the Turkic/Mongolian peoples who invaded Russia in the Middle Ages; hence, not civilized

'ANNA ON THE NECK'

I

After the wedding they had not even light refreshments; the happy pair simply drank a glass of champagne, changed into their travelling things, and drove to the station. Instead of a gay wedding ball and supper, instead of music and dancing, they went on a journey to pray at a shrine a hundred and fifty miles away. Many people commended this, saying that Modest Alexeitch was a man high up in the service and no longer young, and that a noisy wedding might not have seemed quite suitable; and music is apt to sound dreary when a government official of fifty-two marries a girl who is only just eighteen. People said, too, that Modest Alexeitch, being a man of principle, had arranged this visit to the monastery expressly in order to make his young bride realize that even in marriage he put religion and morality above everything.

The happy pair were seen off at the station. The crowd of relations and colleagues in the service stood, with glasses in their hands, waiting for the train to start to shout "Hurrah!" and the bride's father, Pyotr Leontyitch, wearing a top-hat and the uniform of a teacher, already drunk and very pale, kept craning towards the window, glass in hand and saying in an imploring voice:

"Anyuta! Anya, Anya! one word!"

Anna bent out of the window to him, and he whispered something to her, enveloping her in a stale smell of alcohol, blew into her ear —she could make out nothing—and made the sign of the cross over her face, her bosom, and her hands; meanwhile he was breathing in gasps and tears were shining in his eyes. And the schoolboys, Anna's brothers, Petya and Andrusha, pulled at his coat from behind, whispering in confusion:

"Father, hush! . . . Father, that's enough. . . ."

When the train started, Anna saw her father run a little way after the train, staggering and spilling his wine, and what a kind, guilty, pitiful face he had:

"Hurra—ah!" he shouted.

The happy pair were left alone. Modest Alexeitch looked about the compartment, arranged their things on the shelves, and sat down, smiling, opposite his young wife. He was an official of medium height, rather stout and puffy, who looked exceedingly well nourished, with long whiskers and no moustache. His clean-shaven, round, sharply defined chin looked like the heel of a foot. The most characteristic point in his face was the absence of moustache, the bare, freshly shaven place, which gradually passed into the fat cheeks, quivering like jelly. His deportment was dignified, his movements were deliberate, his manner was soft.

"I cannot help remembering now one circumstance," he said, smiling. "When, five years ago, Kosorotov received the order of St. Anna of the second grade, and went to thank His Excellency, His Excellency expressed himself as follows: 'So now you have three Annas: one in your buttonhole and two on your neck.' And it must be explained that at that time Kosorotov's wife, a quarrelsome and frivolous person, had just returned to him, and that her name was Anna. I trust that when I receive the Anna of the second grade His Excellency will not have occasion to say the same thing to me."

He smiled with his little eyes. And she, too, smiled, troubled at the thought that at any moment this man might kiss her with his thick damp lips, and that she had no right to prevent his doing so. The soft movements of his fat person frightened her; she felt both fear and disgust. He got up, without haste took off the order from his neck, took off his coat and waistcoat, and put on his dressing-gown.

"That's better," he said, sitting down beside Anna.

Anna remembered what agony the wedding had been, when it had seemed to her that the priest, and the guests, and every one in church had been looking at her sorrowfully and asking why, why was she, such a sweet, nice girl, marrying such an elderly, uninteresting gentleman. Only that morning she was delighted that everything had been satisfactorily arranged, but at the time of the wedding, and now in the railway carriage, she felt cheated, guilty, and ridiculous. Here she had married a rich man and yet she had no money, her wedding-dress had been bought on credit, and when her father and brothers had been saying good-bye, she could see from their faces that they had not a farthing. Would they have any supper that day? And tomorrow? And for some reason it seemed to her that her father and the boys were sitting tonight hungry without her, and feeling the same misery as they had the day after their mother's funeral.

"Oh, how unhappy I am!" she thought. "Why am I so unhappy?"

With the awkwardness of a man with settled habits, unaccustomed to deal with women, Modest Alexeitch touched her on the waist and patted her on the shoulder, while she went on thinking about money, about her mother and her mother's death. When her mother died, her father, Pyotr Leontyitch, a teacher of drawing and writing in the high school, had taken to drink, impoverishment had followed, the boys had not had boots or goloshes, their father had been hauled up before the magistrate, the warrant officer had come and made an inventory of the furniture. . . . What a disgrace! Anna had had to look after her drunken father, darn her brothers' stockings, go to market, and when she was complimented on her youth, her beauty, and her elegant manners, it seemed to her that every one was looking at her cheap hat and the holes in her boots that were inked over. And at night there had been tears and a haunting dread that her father would soon, very soon, be dismissed from the school for his weakness, and that he would not survive it, but would die, too, like their mother. But ladies of their acquaintance had taken the matter in hand and looked about for a good match for Anna. This Modest Alexevitch, who was neither young nor good-looking but had money, was soon found. He had a hundred thousand in the bank and the family estate, which he had let on lease. He was a man of principle and stood well with His Excellency; it would be nothing to him, so they told Anna, to get a note from His Excellency to the directors of the high school, or even to the Education Commissioner, to prevent Pyotr Leontyitch from being dismissed.

While she was recalling these details, she suddenly heard strains of music which floated in at the window, together with the sound of voices. The train was stopping at a station. In the crowd beyond the platform an accordion and a cheap squeaky fiddle were being briskly played, and the sound of a military band came from beyond the villas and the tall birches and poplars that lay bathed in the moonlight; there must have been a dance in the place. Summer visitors and townspeople, who used to come out here by train in fine weather for a breath of fresh air, were parading up and down on the platform. Among them was the wealthy owner of all the summer villas—a tall, stout, dark man called Artynov. He had prominent eyes and looked like an Armenian. He wore a strange costume; his shirt was unbuttoned, showing his chest; he wore high boots with spurs, and a black cloak hung from his shoulders and dragged on the ground like a train. Two boar-hounds followed him with their sharp noses to the ground.

Tears were still shining in Anna's eyes, but she was not thinking now of her mother, nor of money, nor of her marriage; but shaking hands with schoolboys and officers she knew, she laughed gaily and said quickly:

"How do you do? How are you?"

She went out on to the platform between the carriages into the moonlight, and stood so that they could all see her in her new splendid dress and hat.

"Why are we stopping here?" she asked.

"This is a junction. They are waiting for the mail train to pass."

Seeing that Artynov was looking at her, she screwed up her eyes coquettishly and began talking aloud in French; and because her voice sounded so pleasant, and because she heard music and the moon was reflected in the pond, and because Artynov, the notorious Don Juan and spoiled child of fortune, was looking at her eagerly and with curiosity, and because every one was in good spirits—she suddenly felt joyful, and when the train started and the officers of her acquaintance saluted her, she was humming the polka the strains of which reached her from the military band playing beyond the trees; and she returned to her compartment feeling as though it had been proved to her at the station that she would certainly be happy in spite of everything.

The happy pair spent two days at the monastery, then went back to town. They lived in a rent-free flat. When Modest Alexevitch had gone to the office, Anna played the piano, or shed tears of depression, or lay down on a couch and read novels or looked through fashion papers. At dinner Modest Alexevitch ate a great deal and talked about politics, about appointments, transfers, and promotions in the service, about the necessity of hard work, and said that, family life not being a pleasure but a duty, if you took care of the kopecks the roubles would take care of themselves, and that he put religion and morality before everything else in the world. And holding his knife in his fist as though it were a sword, he would say:

"Every one ought to have his duties!"

And Anna listened to him, was frightened, and could not eat, and she usually got up from the table hungry. After dinner her husband lay down for a nap and snored loudly, while Anna went to see her own people. Her father and the boys looked at her in a peculiar way, as though just before she came in they had been blaming her for having married for money a tedious, wearisome man she did not love; her rustling skirts, her bracelets, and her general air of a married lady, offended them and made them uncomfortable. In her presence they felt a little embarrassed and did not know what to talk to her about; but yet they still loved her as before, and were not used to having dinner without her. She sat down with them to cabbage soup, porridge, and fried potatoes, smelling of mutton dripping. Pyotr Leontyitch filled his glass from the decanter with a trembling hand and drank it off hurriedly, greedily, with repulsion, then poured out a second glass and then a third. Petya and Andrusha, thin, pale boys with big eyes, would take the decanter and say desperately:

"You mustn't, father. . . . Enough, father. . . ."

And Anna, too, was troubled and entreated him to drink no more; and he would suddenly fly into a rage and beat the table with his fists:

"I won't allow any one to dictate to me!" he would shout. "Wretched boys! wretched girl! I'll turn you all out!"

But there was a note of weakness, of good-nature in his voice, and no one was afraid of him. After dinner he usually dressed in his best. Pale, with a cut on his chin from shaving, craning his thin neck, he would stand for half an hour before the glass, prinking, combing his hair, twisting his black moustache, sprinkling himself with scent, tying his cravat in a bow; then he would put on his gloves and his top-hat, and go off to give his private lessons. Or if it was a holiday he would stay at home and paint, or play the harmonium, which wheezed and growled; he would try to wrest from it pure harmonious sounds and would sing to it; or would storm at the boys:

"Wretches! Good-for-nothing boys! You have spoiled the instrument!"

In the evening Anna's husband played cards with his colleagues, who lived under the same roof in the government quarters. The wives of these gentlemen would come in—ugly, tastelessly dressed women, as coarse as cooks—and gossip would begin in the flat as tasteless and unattractive as the ladies themselves. Sometimes Modest Alexevitch would take Anna to the theatre. In the intervals he would never let her stir a step from his side, but walked about arm in arm with her through the corridors and the foyer. When he bowed to some one, he immediately whispered to Anna: "A civil councillor . . . visits at His Excellency's"; or, "A man of means . . . has a house of his own." When they passed the buffet Anna had a great longing for something sweet; she was fond of chocolate and apple cakes, but she had no money, and she did not like to ask her husband. He would take a pear, pinch it with his fingers, and ask uncertainly:

"How much?"

"Twenty-five kopecks!"

"I say!" he would reply, and put it down; but as it was awkward to leave the buffet without buying anything, he would order some seltzer-water and drink the whole bottle himself, and tears would come into his eyes. And Anna hated him at such times.

And suddenly flushing crimson, he would say to her rapidly:

"Bow to that old lady!"

"But I don't know her."

"No matter. That's the wife of the director of the local treasury! Bow, I tell you," he would grumble insistently. "Your head won't drop off."

Anna bowed and her head certainly did not drop off, but it was agonizing. She did everything her husband wanted her to, and was furious with herself for having let him deceive her like the veriest idiot. She had only married him for his money, and yet she had less money now than before her marriage. In old days her father would sometimes give her twenty kopecks, but now she had not a farthing.

To take money by stealth or ask for it, she could not; she was afraid of her husband, she trembled before him. She felt as though she had been afraid of him for years. In her childhood the director of the high school had always seemed the most impressive and terrifying force in the world, sweeping down like a thunderstorm or a steam-engine ready to crush her; another similar force of which the whole family talked, and of which they were for some reason afraid, was His Excellency; then there were a dozen others, less formidable, and among them the teachers at the high school, with shaven upper lips, stern, implacable; and now finally, there was Modest Alexeitch, a man of principle, who even resembled the director in the face. And in Anna's imagination all these forces blended together into one, and, in the form of a terrible, huge white bear, menaced the weak and erring such as her father. And she was afraid to say anything in opposition to her husband, and gave a forced smile, and tried to make a show of pleasure when she was coarsely caressed and defiled by embraces that excited her terror. Only once Pyotr Leontyitch had the temerity to ask for a loan of fifty roubles in order to pay some very irksome debt, but what an agony it had been!

"Very good; I'll give it to you," said Modest Alexeitch after a moment's thought; "but I warn you I won't help you again till you give up drinking. Such a failing is disgraceful in a man in the government service! I must remind you of the well-known fact that many capable people have been ruined by that passion, though they might possibly, with temperance, have risen in time to a very high."

And long-winded phrases followed: "inasmuch as . . .", "following upon which proposition . . .", "in view of the aforesaid contention . . ."; and Pyotr Leontyitch was in agonies of humiliation and felt an intense craving for alcohol.

And when the boys came to visit Anna, generally in broken boots and threadbare trousers, they, too, had to listen to sermons.

"Every man ought to have his duties!" Modest Alexeitch would say to them.

And he did not give them money. But he did give Anna bracelets, rings, and brooches, saying that these things would come in useful for a rainy day. And he often unlocked her drawer and made an inspection to see whether they were all safe.

II

Meanwhile winter came on. Long before Christmas there was an announcement in the local papers that the usual winter ball would take place on the twenty-ninth of December in the Hall of Nobility. Every evening after cards Modest Alexeitch was excitedly whispering with his colleagues' wives and glancing at Anna, and then paced up and down the room for a long while, thinking. At last, late one evening, he stood still, facing Anna, and said:

"You ought to get yourself a ball dress. Do you understand? Only please consult Marya Grigoryevna and Natalya Kuzminishna."

And he gave her a hundred roubles. She took the money, but she did not consult any one when she ordered the ball dress; she spoke to no one but her father, and tried to imagine how her mother would have dressed for a ball. Her mother had always dressed in the latest fashion and had always taken trouble over Anna, dressing her elegantly like a doll, and had taught her to speak French and dance the mazurka superbly (she had been a governess for five years before her marriage). Like her mother, Anna could make a new dress out of an old one, clean gloves with benzine, hire jewels; and, like her mother, she knew how to screw up her eyes, lisp, assume graceful attitudes, fly into raptures when necessary, and throw a mournful and enigmatic look into her eyes. And from her father she had inherited the dark colour of her hair and eyes, her highly-strung nerves, and the habit of always making herself look her best.

When, half an hour before setting off for the ball, Modest Alexeitch went into her room without his coat on, to put his order round his neck before her pier-glass, dazzled by her beauty and the splendour of her fresh, ethereal dress, he combed his whiskers complacently and said:

"So that's what my wife can look like . . . so that's what you can look like! Anyuta!" he went on, dropping into a tone of solemnity, "I have made your fortune, and now I beg you to do something for mine. I beg you to get introduced to the wife of His Excellency! For God's sake, do! Through her I may get the post of senior reporting clerk!"

They went to the ball. They reached the Hall of Nobility, the entrance with the hall porter. They came to the vestibule with the hat-stands, the fur coats; footmen scurrying about, and ladies with low necks putting up their fans to screen themselves from the draughts. There was a smell of gas and of soldiers. When Anna, walking upstairs on her husband's arm, heard the music and saw herself full length in the looking-glass in the full glow of the lights, there was a rush of joy in her heart, and she felt the same presentiment of happiness as in the moonlight at the station. She walked in proudly, confidently, for the first time feeling herself not a girl but a lady, and unconsciously imitating her mother in her walk and in her manner. And for the first time in her life she felt rich and free. Even her husband's presence did not oppress her, for as she crossed the threshold of the hall she had guessed instinctively that the proximity of an old husband did not detract from her in the least, but, on the contrary, gave her that shade of piquant mystery that is so attractive to men. The orchestra was already playing and the dances had begun. After their flat Anna was overwhelmed by the lights, the bright colours, the music, the noise, and looking round the room, thought, "Oh, how lovely!" She at once distinguished in the crowd all her acquaintances, every one she had met before at parties or on picnics—all the officers, the teachers, the lawyers, the officials, the landowners, His Excellency, Artynov, and the ladies of the highest standing, dressed up and verydécollettées, handsome and ugly, who had already taken up their positions in the stalls and pavilions of the charity bazaar, to begin selling things for the benefit of the poor. A huge officer in epaulettes—she had been introduced to him in Staro-Kievsky Street when she was a schoolgirl, but now she could not remember his name—seemed to spring from out of the ground, begging her for a waltz, and she flew away from her husband, feeling as though she were floating away in a sailing-boat in a violent storm, while her husband was left far away on the shore. She danced passionately, with fervour, a waltz, then a polka and a quadrille, being snatched by one partner as soon as she was left by another, dizzy with music and the noise, mixing Russian with French, lisping, laughing, and with no thought of her husband or anything else. She excited great admiration among the men—that was evident, and indeed it could not have been otherwise; she was breathless with excitement, felt thirsty, and convulsively clutched her fan. Pyotr Leontyitch, her father, in a crumpled dress-coat that smelt of benzine, came up to her, offering her a plate of pink ice.

"You are enchanting this evening," he said, looking at her rapturously, "and I have never so much regretted that you were in such a hurry to get married. . . . What was it for? I know you did it for our sake, but . . ." With a shaking hand he drew out a roll of notes and said: "I got the money for my lessons today, and can pay your husband what I owe him."

She put the plate back into his hand, and was pounced upon by some one and borne off to a distance. She caught a glimpse over her partner's shoulder of her father gliding over the floor, putting his arm round a lady and whirling down the ball-room with her.

"How sweet he is when he is sober!" she thought.

She danced the mazurka with the same huge officer; he moved gravely, as heavily as a dead carcase in a uniform, twitched his shoulders and his chest, stamped his feet very languidly—he felt fearfully disinclined to dance. She fluttered round him, provoking him by her beauty, her bare neck; her eyes glowed defiantly, her movements were passionate, while he became more and more indifferent, and held out his hands to her as graciously as a king.

"Bravo, bravo!" said people watching them.

But little by little the huge officer, too, broke out; he grew lively, excited, and, overcome by her fascination, was carried away and danced lightly, youthfully, while she merely moved her shoulders and looked slyly at him as though she were now the queen and he were her slave; and at that moment it seemed to her that the whole room was looking at them, and that everybody was thrilled and envied them. The huge officer had hardly had time to thank her for the dance, when the crowd suddenly parted and the men drew themselves up in a strange way, with their hands at their sides.

His Excellency, with two stars on his dress-coat, was walking up to her. Yes, His Excellency was walking straight towards her, for he was staring directly at her with a sugary smile, while he licked his lips as he always did when he saw a pretty woman.

"Delighted, delighted . . ." he began. "I shall order your husband to be clapped in a lock-up for keeping such a treasure hidden from us till now. I've come to you with a message from my wife," he went on, offering her his arm. "You must help us. . . . M-m-yes. . . . We ought to give you the prize for beauty as they do in America . . . . M-m-yes. . . . The Americans. . . . My wife is expecting you impatiently."

He led her to a stall and presented her to a middle-aged lady, the lower part of whose face was disproportionately large, so that she looked as though she were holding a big stone in her mouth.

"You must help us," she said through her nose in a sing-song voice. "All the pretty women are working for our charity bazaar, and you are the only one enjoying yourself. Why won't you help us?"

She went away, and Anna took her place by the cups and the silver samovar. She was soon doing a lively trade. Anna asked no less than a rouble for a cup of tea, and made the huge officer drink three cups. Artynov, the rich man with prominent eyes, who suffered from asthma, came up, too; he was not dressed in the strange costume in which Anna had seen him in the summer at the station, but wore a dress-coat like every one else. Keeping his eyes fixed on Anna, he drank a glass of champagne and paid a hundred roubles for it, then drank some tea and gave another hundred—all this without saying a word, as he was short of breath through asthma. . . . Anna invited purchasers and got money out of them, firmly convinced by now that her smiles and glances could not fail to afford these people great pleasure. She realized now that she was created exclusively for this noisy, brilliant, laughing life, with its music, its dancers, its adorers, and her old terror of a force that was sweeping down upon her and menacing to crush her seemed to her ridiculous: she was afraid of no one now, and only regretted that her mother could not be there to rejoice at her success.

Pyotr Leontyitch, pale by now but still steady on his legs, came up to the stall and asked for a glass of brandy. Anna turned crimson, expecting him to say something inappropriate (she was already ashamed of having such a poor and ordinary father); but he emptied his glass, took ten roubles out of his roll of notes, flung it down, and walked away with dignity without uttering a word. A little later she saw him dancing in the grand chain, and by now he was staggering and kept shouting something, to the great confusion of his partner; and Anna remembered how at the ball three years before he had staggered and shouted in the same way, and it had ended in the police-sergeant's taking him home to bed, and next day the director had threatened to dismiss him from his post. How inappropriate that memory was!

When the samovars were put out in the stalls and the exhausted ladies handed over their takings to the middle-aged lady with the stone in her mouth, Artynov took Anna on his arm to the hall where supper was served to all who had assisted at the bazaar. There were some twenty people at supper, not more, but it was very noisy. His Excellency proposed a toast:

"In this magnificent dining-room it will be appropriate to drink to the success of the cheap dining-rooms, which are the object of today's bazaar."

The brigadier-general proposed the toast: "To the power by which even the artillery is vanquished," and all the company clinked glasses with the ladies. It was very, very gay.

When Anna was escorted home it was daylight and the cooks were going to market. Joyful, intoxicated, full of new sensations, exhausted, she undressed, dropped into bed, and at once fell asleep. . . .

It was past one in the afternoon when the servant waked her and announced that M. Artynov had called. She dressed quickly and went down into the drawing-room. Soon after Artynov, His Excellency called to thank her for her assistance in the bazaar. With a sugary smile, chewing his lips, he kissed her hand, and asking her permission to come again, took his leave, while she remained standing in the middle of the drawing-room, amazed, enchanted, unable to believe that this change in her life, this marvellous change, had taken place so quickly; and at that moment Modest Alexeitch walked in . . . and he, too, stood before her now with the same ingratiating, sugary, cringingly respectful expression which she was accustomed to see on his face in the presence of the great and powerful; and with rapture, with indignation, with contempt, convinced that no harm would come to her from it, she said, articulating distinctly each word:

"Be off, you blockhead!"

From this time forward Anna never had one day free, as she was always taking part in picnics, expeditions, performances. She returned home every day after midnight, and went to bed on the floor in the drawing-room, and afterwards used to tell every one, touchingly, how she slept under flowers. She needed a very great deal of money, but she was no longer afraid of Modest Alexeitch, and spent his money as though it were her own; and she did not ask, did not demand it, simply sent him in the bills. "Give bearer two hundred roubles," or "Pay one hundred roubles at once."

At Easter Modest Alexeitch received the Anna of the second grade. When he went to offer his thanks, His Excellency put aside the paper he was reading and settled himself more comfortably in his chair.

"So now you have three Annas," he said, scrutinizing his white hands and pink nails—"one on your buttonhole and two on your neck."

Modest Alexeitch put two fingers to his lips as a precaution against laughing too loud and said:

"Now I have only to look forward to the arrival of a little Vladimir. I make bold to beg your Excellency to stand godfather."

He was alluding to Vladimir of the fourth grade, and was already imagining how he would tell everywhere the story of this pun, so happy in its readiness and audacity, and he wanted to say something equally happy, but His Excellency was buried again in his newspaper, and merely gave him a nod.

And Anna went on driving about with three horses, going out hunting with Artynov, playing in one-act dramas, going out to supper, and was more and more rarely with her own family; they dined now alone. Pyotr Leontyitch was drinking more heavily than ever; there was no money, and the harmonium had been sold long ago for debt. The boys did not let him go out alone in the street now, but looked after him for fear he might fall down; and whenever they met Anna driving in Staro-Kievsky Street with a pair of horses and Artynov on the box instead of a coachman, Pyotr Leontyitch took off his top-hat, and was about to shout to her, but Petya and Andrusha took him by the arm, and said imploringly:

"You mustn't, father. Hush, father!"

NOTES

journey: it cost much less to stay at the monestary guest-houses than at a hotel; this is the first indication of Modest Alexeitch's stinginess

uniform of a teacher: both teachers and students in Chekhov's Russia wore uniforms

the order of St. Anna: Russian decorations came in different grades; lower grades would be placed in a buttonhole, while higher grades were pinned on the chest or hung around the neck

screwed up her eyes: action that Russians considered flirtatious

intervals: intermissions

Hall of Nobility: a club and meeting place for the gentry in a Russian provincial town

décollettées: cut low at the neckline, fashionable

with three horses: a pretentious style of driving about

THE TEACHER OF LITERATURE

I

There was the thud of horses' hoofs on the wooden floor; they brought out of the stable the black horse, Count Nulin; then the white, Giant; then his sister Maika. They were all magnificent, expensive horses. Old Shelestov saddled Giant and said, addressing his daughter Masha:

"Well, Marie Godefroi, come, get on! Hopla!"

Masha Shelestov was the youngest of the family; she was eighteen, but her family could not get used to thinking that she was not a little girl, and so they still called her Manya and Manyusa; and after there had been a circus in the town which she had eagerly visited, every one began to call her Marie Godefroi.

"Hop-la!" she cried, mounting Giant. Her sister Varya got on Maika, Nikitin on Count Nulin, the officers on their horses, and the long picturesque cavalcade, with the officers in white tunics and the ladies in their riding habits, moved at a walking pace out of the yard.

Nikitin noticed that when they were mounting the horses and afterwards riding out into the street, Masha for some reason paid attention to no one but himself. She looked anxiously at him and at Count Nulin and said:

"You must hold him all the time on the curb, Sergey Vassilitch. Don't let him shy. He's pretending."

And either because her Giant was very friendly with Count Nulin, or perhaps by chance, she rode all the time beside Nikitin, as she had done the day before, and the day before that. And he looked at her graceful little figure sitting on the proud white beast, at her delicate profile, at the chimney-pot hat, which did not suit her at all and made her look older than her age—looked at her with joy, with tenderness, with rapture; listened to her, taking in little of what she said, and thought:

"I promise on my honour, I swear to God, I won't be afraid and I'll speak to her today."

It was seven o'clock in the evening—the time when the scent of white acacia and lilac is so strong that the air and the very trees seem heavy with the fragrance. The band was already playing in the town gardens. The horses made a resounding thud on the pavement, on all sides there were sounds of laughter, talk, and the banging of gates. The soldiers they met saluted the officers, the schoolboys bowed to Nikitin, and all the people who were hurrying to the gardens to hear the band were pleased at the sight of the party. And how warm it was! How soft-looking were the clouds scattered carelessly about the sky, how kindly and comforting the shadows of the poplars and the acacias, which stretched across the street and reached as far as the balconies and second stories of the houses on the other side.

They rode on out of the town and set off at a trot along the high-road. Here there was no scent of lilac and acacia, no music of the band, but there was the fragrance of the fields, there was the green of young rye and wheat, the marmots were squeaking, the rooks were cawing. Wherever one looked it was green, with only here and there black patches of bare ground, and far away to the left in the cemetery a white streak of apple-blossom.

They passed the slaughter-houses, then the brewery, and over-took a military band hastening to the suburban gardens.

"Polyansky has a very fine horse, I don't deny that," Masha said to Nikitin, with a glance towards the officer who was riding beside Varya. "But it has blemishes. That white patch on its left leg ought not to be there, and, look, it tosses its head. You can't train it not to now; it will toss its head till the end of its days."

Masha was as passionate a lover of horses as her father. She felt a pang when she saw other people with fine horses, and was pleased when she saw defects in them. Nikitin knew nothing about horses; it made absolutely no difference to him whether he held his horse on the bridle or on the curb, whether he trotted or galloped; he only felt that his position was strained and unnatural, and that consequently the officers who knew how to sit in their saddles must please Masha more than he could. And he was jealous of the officers.

As they rode by the suburban gardens some one suggested their going in and getting some seltzer-water. They went in. There were no trees but oaks in the gardens; they had only just come into leaf, so that through the young foliage the whole garden could still be seen with its platform, little tables, and swings, and the crows' nests were visible, looking like big hats. The party dismounted near a table and asked for seltzer-water. People they knew, walking about the garden, came up to them. Among them the army doctor in high boots, and the conductor of the band, waiting for the musicians. The doctor must have taken Nikitin for a student, for he asked: "Have you come for the summer holidays?"

"No, I am here permanently," answered Nikitin. "I am a teacher at the school."

"You don't say so?" said the doctor, with surprise. "So young and already a teacher?"

"Young, indeed! My goodness, I'm twenty-six!

"You have a beard and moustache, but yet one would never guess you were more than twenty-two or twenty-three. How young-looking you are!"

"What a beast!" thought Nikitin. "He, too, takes me for a whipper-snapper!"

He disliked it extremely when people referred to his youth, especially in the presence of women or the schoolboys. Ever since he had come to the town as a master in the school he had detested his own youthful appearance. The schoolboys were not afraid of him, old people called him "young man," ladies preferred dancing with him to listening to his long arguments, and he would have given a great deal to be ten years older.

From the garden they went on to the Shelestovs' farm. There they stopped at the gate and asked the bailiff's wife, Praskovya, to bring some new milk. Nobody drank the milk; they all looked at one another, laughed, and galloped back. As they rode back the band was playing in the suburban garden; the sun was setting behind the cemetery, and half the sky was crimson from the sunset.

Masha again rode beside Nikitin. He wanted to tell her how passionately he loved her, but he was afraid he would be overheard by the officers and Varya, and he was silent. Masha was silent, too, and he felt why she was silent and why she was riding beside him, and was so happy that the earth, the sky, the lights of the town, the black outline of the brewery—all blended for him into something very pleasant and comforting, and it seemed to him as though Count Nulin were stepping on air and would climb up into the crimson sky.

They arrived home. The samovar was already boiling on the table, old Shelestov was sitting with his friends, officials in the Circuit Court, and as usual he was criticizing something.

"It's loutishness!" he said. "Loutishness and nothing more. Yes!"

Since Nikitin had been in love with Masha, everything at the Shelestovs' pleased him: the house, the garden, and the evening tea, and the wickerwork chairs, and the old nurse, and even the word "loutishness," which the old man was fond of using. The only thing he did not like was the number of cats and dogs and the Egyptian pigeons, who moaned disconsolately in a big cage in the verandah. There were so many house-dogs and yard-dogs that he had only learnt to recognize two of them in the course of his acquaintance with the Shelestovs: Mushka and Som. Mushka was a little mangy dog with a shaggy face, spiteful and spoiled. She hated Nikitin: when she saw him she put her head on one side, showed her teeth, and began: "Rrr . . . nga-nga-nga . . . rrr . . . !" Then she would get under his chair, and when he would try to drive her away she would go off into piercing yaps, and the family would say: "Don't be frightened. She doesn't bite. She is a good dog."

Som was a tall black dog with long legs and a tail as hard as a stick. At dinner and tea he usually moved about under the table, and thumped on people's boots and on the legs of the table with his tail. He was a good-natured, stupid dog, but Nikitin could not endure him because he had the habit of putting his head on people's knees at dinner and messing their trousers with saliva. Nikitin had more than once tried to hit him on his head with a knife-handle, to flip him on the nose, had abused him, had complained of him, but nothing saved his trousers.

After their ride the tea, jam, rusks, and butter seemed very nice. They all drank their first glass in silence and with great relish; over the second they began an argument. It was always Varya who started the arguments at tea; she was good-looking, handsomer than Masha, and was considered the cleverest and most cultured person in the house, and she behaved with dignity and severity, as an eldest daughter should who has taken the place of her dead mother in the house. As the mistress of the house, she felt herself entitled to wear a dressing-gown in the presence of her guests, and to call the officers by their surnames; she looked on Masha as a little girl, and talked to her as though she were a schoolmistress. She used to speak of herself as an old maid—so she was certain she would marry.

Every conversation, even about the weather, she invariably turned into an argument. She had a passion for catching at words, pouncing on contradictions, quibbling over phrases. You would begin talking to her, and she would stare at you and suddenly interrupt: "Excuse me, excuse me, Petrov, the other day you said the very opposite!"

Or she would smile ironically and say: "I notice, though, you begin to advocate the principles of the secret police. I congratulate you."

If you jested or made a pun, you would hear her voice at once: "That's stale," "That's pointless." If an officer ventured on a joke, she would make a contemptuous grimace and say, "An army joke!"

And she rolled the r so impressively that Mushka invariably answered from under a chair, "Rrr . . . nga-nga-nga . . . !"

On this occasion at tea the argument began with Nikitin's mentioning the school examinations.

"Excuse me, Sergey Vassilitch," Varya interrupted him. "You say it's difficult for the boys. And whose fault is that, let me ask you? For instance, you set the boys in the eighth class an essay on 'Pushkin as a Psychologist.' To begin with, you shouldn't set such a difficult subject; and, secondly, Pushkin was not a psychologist. Shtchedrin now, or Dostoevsky let us say, is a different matter, but Pushkin is a great poet and nothing more."

"Shtchedrin is one thing, and Pushkin is another," Nikitin answered sulkily.

"I know you don't think much of Shtchedrin at the high school, but that's not the point. Tell me, in what sense is Pushkin a psychologist?"

"Why, do you mean to say he was not a psychologist? If you like, I'll give you examples."

And Nikitin recited several passages from "Onyegin" and then from "Boris Godunov."

"I see no psychology in that." Varya sighed. "The psychologist is the man who describes the recesses of the human soul, and that's fine poetry and nothing more."

"I know the sort of psychology you want," said Nikitin, offended. "You want some one to saw my finger with a blunt saw while I howl at the top of my voice—that's what you mean by psychology."

"That's poor! But still you haven't shown me in what sense Pushkin is a psychologist?"

When Nikitin had to argue against anything that seemed to him narrow, conventional, or something of that kind, he usually leaped up from his seat, clutched at his head with both hands, and began with a moan, running from one end of the room to another. And it was the same now: he jumped up, clutched his head in his hands, and with a moan walked round the table, then he sat down a little way off.

The officers took his part. Captain Polyansky began assuring Varya that Pushkin really was a psychologist, and to prove it quoted two lines from Lermontov; Lieutenant Gernet said that if Pushkin had not been a psychologist they would not have erected a monument to him in Moscow.

"That's loutishness!" was heard from the other end of the table. "I said as much to the governor: 'It's loutishness, your Excellency,' I said."

"I won't argue any more," cried Nikitin. "It's unending. . . . Enough! Ach, get away, you nasty dog!" he cried to Som, who laid his head and paw on his knee.

"Rrr . . . nga-nga-nga!" came from under the table.

"Admit that you are wrong!" cried Varya. "Own up!"

But some young ladies came in, and the argument dropped of itself. They all went into the drawing-room. Varya sat down at the piano and began playing dances. They danced first a waltz, then a polka, then a quadrille with a grand chain which Captain Polyansky led through all the rooms, then a waltz again.

During the dancing the old men sat in the drawing-room, smoking and looking at the young people. Among them was Shebaldin, the director of the municipal bank, who was famed for his love of literature and dramatic art. He had founded the local Musical and Dramatic Society, and took part in the performances himself, confining himself, for some reason, to playing comic footmen or to reading in a sing-song voice "The Woman who was a Sinner." His nickname in the town was "the Mummy," as he was tall, very lean and scraggy, and always had a solemn air and a fixed, lustreless eye. He was so devoted to the dramatic art that he even shaved his moustache and beard, and this made him still more like a mummy.

After the grand chain, he shuffled up to Nikitin sideways, coughed, and said:

"I had the pleasure of being present during the argument at tea. I fully share your opinion. We are of one mind, and it would be a great pleasure to me to talk to you. Have you read Lessing on the dramatic art of Hamburg?"

"No, I haven't."

Shebaldin was horrified, and waved his hands as though he had burnt his fingers, and saying nothing more, staggered back from Nikitin. Shebaldin's appearance, his question, and his surprise, struck Nikitin as funny, but he thought none the less:

"It really is awkward. I am a teacher of literature, and to this day I've not read Lessing. I must read him."

Before supper the whole company, old and young, sat down to play "fate." They took two packs of cards: one pack was dealt round to the company, the other was laid on the table face downwards.

"The one who has this card in his hand," old Shelestov began solemnly, lifting the top card of the second pack, "is fated to go into the nursery and kiss nurse."

The pleasure of kissing the nurse fell to the lot of Shebaldin. They all crowded round him, took him to the nursery, and laughing and clapping their hands, made him kiss the nurse. There was a great uproar and shouting.

"Not so ardently!" cried Shelestov with tears of laughter. "Not so ardently!"

It was Nikitin's "fate" to hear the confessions of all. He sat on a chair in the middle of the drawing-room. A shawl was brought and put over his head. The first who came to confess to him was Varya.

"I know your sins," Nikitin began, looking in the darkness at her stern profile. "Tell me, madam, how do you explain your walking with Polyansky every day? Oh, it's not for nothing she walks with an hussar!"

"That's poor," said Varya, and walked away.

Then under the shawl he saw the shine of big motionless eyes, caught the lines of a dear profile in the dark, together with a familiar, precious fragrance which reminded Nikitin of Masha's room.

"Marie Godefroi," he said, and did not know his own voice, it was so soft and tender, "what are your sins?"

Masha screwed up her eyes and put out the tip of her tongue at him, then she laughed and went away. And a minute later she was standing in the middle of the room, clapping her hands and crying:

"Supper, supper, supper!"

And they all streamed into the dining-room. At supper Varya had another argument, and this time with her father. Polyansky ate stolidly, drank red wine, and described to Nikitin how once in a winter campaign he had stood all night up to his knees in a bog; the enemy was so near that they were not allowed to speak or smoke, the night was cold and dark, a piercing wind was blowing. Nikitin listened and stole side-glances at Masha. She was gazing at him immovably, without blinking, as though she was pondering something or was lost in a reverie. . . . It was pleasure and agony to him both at once.

"Why does she look at me like that?" was the question that fretted him. "It's awkward. People may notice it. Oh, how young, how naïve she is!"

The party broke up at midnight. When Nikitin went out at the gate, a window opened on the first-floor, and Masha showed herself at it.

"Sergey Vassilitch!" she called.

"What is it?"

"I tell you what . . ." said Masha, evidently thinking of something to say. "I tell you what. . . Polyansky said he would come in a day or two with his camera and take us all. We must meet here."

"Very well."

Masha vanished, the window was slammed, and some one immediately began playing the piano in the house.

"Well, it is a house!" thought Nikitin while he crossed the street. "A house in which there is no moaning except from Egyptian pigeons, and they only do it because they have no other means of expressing their joy!"

But the Shelestovs were not the only festive household. Nikitin had not gone two hundred paces before he heard the strains of a piano from another house. A little further he met a peasant playing the balalaika at the gate. In the gardens the band struck up a potpourri of Russian songs.

Nikitin lived nearly half a mile from the Shelestoys' in a flat of eight rooms at the rent of three hundred roubles a year, which he shared with his colleague Ippolit Ippolititch, a teacher of geography and history. When Nikitin went in this Ippolit Ippolititch, a snub-nosed, middle-aged man with a reddish beard, with a coarse, good-natured, unintellectual face like a workman's, was sitting at the table correcting his pupils' maps. He considered that the most important and necessary part of the study of geography was the drawing of maps, and of the study of history the learning of dates: he would sit for nights together correcting in blue pencil the maps drawn by the boys and girls he taught, or making chronological tables.

"What a lovely day it has been!" said Nikitin, going in to him. "I wonder at you—how can you sit indoors?"

Ippolit Ippolititch was not a talkative person; he either remained silent or talked of things which everybody knew already. Now what he answered was:

"Yes, very fine weather. It's May now; we soon shall have real summer. And summer's a very different thing from winter. In the winter you have to heat the stoves, but in summer you can keep warm without. In summer you have your window open at night and still are warm, and in winter you are cold even with the double frames in."

Nikitin had not sat at the table for more than one minute before he was bored.

"Good-night!" he said, getting up and yawning. "I wanted to tell you something romantic concerning myself, but you are—geography! If one talks to you of love, you will ask one at once, 'What was the date of the Battle of Kalka?' Confound you, with your battles and your capes in Siberia!"

"What are you cross about?"

"Why, it is vexatious!"

And vexed that he had not spoken to Masha, and that he had no one to talk to of his love, he went to his study and lay down upon the sofa. It was dark and still in the study. Lying gazing into the darkness, Nikitin for some reason began thinking how in two or three years he would go to Petersburg, how Masha would see him off at the station and would cry; in Petersburg he would get a long letter from her in which she would entreat him to come home as quickly as possible. And he would write to her. . . . He would begin his letter like that: "My dear little rat!"

"Yes, my dear little rat!" he said, and he laughed.

He was lying in an uncomfortable position. He put his arms under his head and put his left leg over the back of the sofa. He felt more comfortable. Meanwhile a pale light was more and more perceptible at the windows, sleepy cocks crowed in the yard. Nikitin went on thinking how he would come back from Petersburg, how Masha would meet him at the station, and with a shriek of delight would fling herself on his neck; or, better still, he would cheat her and come home by stealth late at night: the cook would open the door, then he would go on tiptoe to the bedroom, undress noiselessly, and jump into bed! And she would wake up and be overjoyed.

It was beginning to get quite light. By now there were no windows, no study. On the steps of the brewery by which they had ridden that day Masha was sitting, saying something. Then she took Nikitin by the arm and went with him to the suburban garden. There he saw the oaks and, the crows' nests like hats. One of the nests rocked; out of it peeped Shebaldin, shouting loudly: "You have not read Lessing!"

Nikitin shuddered all over and opened his eyes. Ippolit Ippolititch was standing before the sofa, and throwing back his head, was putting on his cravat.

"Get up; it's time for school," he said. "You shouldn't sleep in your clothes; it spoils your clothes. You should sleep in your bed, undressed."

And as usual he began slowly and emphatically saying what everybody knew.

Nikitin's first lesson was on Russian language in the second class. When at nine o'clock punctually he went into the classroom, he saw written on the blackboard two large letters—M. S. That, no doubt, meant Masha Shelestov.

"They've scented it out already, the rascals . . ." thought Nikitin. "How is it they know everything?"

The second lesson was in the fifth class. And there two letters, M. S., were written on the blackboard; and when he went out of the classroom at the end of the lesson, he heard the shout behind him as though from a theatre gallery:

"Hurrah for Masha Shelestov!"

His head was heavy from sleeping in his clothes, his limbs were weighted down with inertia. The boys, who were expecting every day to break up before the examinations, did nothing, were restless, and so bored that they got into mischief. Nikitin, too, was restless, did not notice their pranks, and was continually going to the window. He could see the street brilliantly lighted up with the sun; above the houses the blue limpid sky, the birds, and far, far away, beyond the gardens and the houses, vast indefinite distance, the forests in the blue haze, the smoke from a passing train. . . .

Here two officers in white tunics, playing with their whips, passed in the street in the shade of the acacias. Here a lot of Jews, with grey beards, and caps on, drove past in a waggonette. . . . The governess walked by with the director's granddaughter. Som ran by in the company of two other dogs. . . . And then Varya, wearing a simple grey dress and red stockings, carrying the "Vyestnik Evropi" in her hand, passed by. She must have been to the town library. . . .

And it would be a long time before lessons were over at three o'clock! And after school he could not go home nor to the Shelestovs', but must go to give a lesson at Wolf's. This Wolf, a wealthy Jew who had turned Lutheran, did not send his children to the high school, but had them taught at home by the high-school masters, and paid five roubles a lesson.

He was bored, bored, bored.

At three o'clock he went to Wolf's and spent there, as it seemed to him, an eternity. He left there at five o'clock, and before seven he had to be at the high school again to a meeting of the masters —to draw up the plan for the viva voce examination of the fourth and sixth classes.

When late in the evening he left the high school and went to the Shelestovs', his heart was beating and his face was flushed. A month before, even a week before, he had, every time that he made up his mind to speak to her, prepared a whole speech, with an introduction and a conclusion. Now he had not one word ready; everything was in a muddle in his head, and all he knew was that today he would certainly declare himself, and that it was utterly impossible to wait any longer.

"I will ask her to come to the garden," he thought; "we'll walk about a little and I'll speak."

There was not a soul in the hall; he went into the dining-room and then into the drawing-room. . . . There was no one there either. He could hear Varya arguing with some one upstairs and the clink of the dressmaker's scissors in the nursery.

There was a little room in the house which had three names: the little room, the passage room, and the dark room. There was a big cupboard in it where they kept medicines, gunpowder, and their hunting gear. Leading from this room to the first floor was a narrow wooden staircase where cats were always asleep. There were two doors in it—one leading to the nursery, one to the drawing-room. When Nikitin went into this room to go upstairs, the door from the nursery opened and shut with such a bang that it made the stairs and the cupboard tremble; Masha, in a dark dress, ran in with a piece of blue material in her hand, and, not noticing Nikitin, darted towards the stairs.

"Stay . . ." said Nikitin, stopping her. "Good-evening, Godefroi . . . . Allow me. . . ."

He gasped, he did not know what to say; with one hand he held her hand and with the other the blue material. And she was half frightened, half surprised, and looked at him with big eyes.

"Allow me . . ." Nikitin went on, afraid she would go away. "There's something I must say to you. . . . Only . . . it's inconvenient here. I cannot, I am incapable. . . . Understand, Godefroi, I can't —that's all . . . ."

The blue material slipped on to the floor, and Nikitin took Masha by the other hand. She turned pale, moved her lips, then stepped back from Nikitin and found herself in the corner between the wall and the cupboard.

"On my honour, I assure you . . ." he said softly. "Masha, on my honour. . . ."

She threw back her head and he kissed her lips, and that the kiss might last longer he put his fingers to her cheeks; and it somehow happened that he found himself in the corner between the cupboard and the wall, and she put her arms round his neck and pressed her head against his chin.

Then they both ran into the garden. The Shelestoys had a garden of nine acres. There were about twenty old maples and lime-trees in it; there was one fir-tree, and all the rest were fruit-trees: cherries, apples, pears, horse-chestnuts, silvery olive-trees. . . . There were heaps of flowers, too.

Nikitin and Masha ran along the avenues in silence, laughed, asked each other from time to time disconnected questions which they did not answer. A crescent moon was shining over the garden, and drowsy tulips and irises were stretching up from the dark grass in its faint light, as though entreating for words of love for them, too.

When Nikitin and Masha went back to the house, the officers and the young ladies were already assembled and dancing the mazurka. Again Polyansky led the grand chain through all the rooms, again after dancing they played "fate." Before supper, when the visitors had gone into the dining-room, Masha, left alone with Nikitin, pressed close to him and said:

"You must speak to papa and Varya yourself; I am ashamed."

After supper he talked to the old father. After listening to him, Shelestov thought a little and said:

"I am very grateful for the honour you do me and my daughter, but let me speak to you as a friend. I will speak to you, not as a father, but as one gentleman to another. Tell me, why do you want to be married so young? Only peasants are married so young, and that, of course, is loutishness. But why should you? Where's the satisfaction of putting on the fetters at your age?"

"I am not young!" said Nikitin, offended. "I am in my twenty-seventh year."

"Papa, the farrier has come!" cried Varya from the other room.

And the conversation broke off. Varya, Masha, and Polyansky saw Nikitin home. When they reached his gate, Varya said:

"Why is it your mysterious Metropolit Metropolititch never shows himself anywhere? He might come and see us."

The mysterious Ippolit Ippolititch was sitting on his bed, taking off his trousers, when Nikitin went in to him.

"Don't go to bed, my dear fellow," said Nikitin breathlessly. "Stop a minute; don't go to bed!"

Ippolit Ippolititch put on his trousers hurriedly and asked in a flutter:

"What is it?"

"I am going to be married."

Nikitin sat down beside his companion, and looking at him wonderingly, as though surprised at himself, said:

"Only fancy, I am going to be married! To Masha Shelestov! I made an offer today."

"Well? She seems a good sort of girl. Only she is very young."

"Yes, she is young," sighed Nikitin, and shrugged his shoulders with a careworn air. "Very, very young!"

"She was my pupil at the high school. I know her. She wasn't bad at geography, but she was no good at history. And she was inattentive in class, too."

Nikitin for some reason felt suddenly sorry for his companion, and longed to say something kind and comforting to him.

"My dear fellow, why don't you get married?" he asked. "Why don't you marry Varya, for instance? She is a splendid, first-rate girl! It's true she is very fond of arguing, but a heart . . . what a heart! She was just asking about you. Marry her, my dear boy! Eh?"

He knew perfectly well that Varya would not marry this dull, snub-nosed man, but still persuaded him to marry her—why?

"Marriage is a serious step," said Ippolit Ippolititch after a moment's thought. "One has to look at it all round and weigh things thoroughly; it's not to be done rashly. Prudence is always a good thing, and especially in marriage, when a man, ceasing to be a bachelor, begins a new life."

And he talked of what every one has known for ages. Nikitin did not stay to listen, said goodnight, and went to his own room. He undressed quickly and quickly got into bed, in order to be able to think the sooner of his happiness, of Masha, of the future; he smiled, then suddenly recalled that he had not read Lessing.

"I must read him," he thought. "Though, after all, why should I? Bother him!"

And exhausted by his happiness, he fell asleep at once and went on smiling till the morning.

He dreamed of the thud of horses' hoofs on a wooden floor; he dreamed of the black horse Count Nulin, then of the white Giant and its sister Maika, being led out of the stable.

II

"It was very crowded and noisy in the church, and once some one cried out, and the head priest, who was marrying Masha and me, looked through his spectacles at the crowd, and said severely: 'Don't move about the church, and don't make a noise, but stand quietly and pray. You should have the fear of God in your hearts.'

"My best men were two of my colleagues, and Masha's best men were Captain Polyansky and Lieutenant Gernet. The bishop's choir sang superbly. The sputtering of the candles, the brilliant light, the gorgeous dresses, the officers, the numbers of gay, happy faces, and a special ethereal look in Masha, everything together—the surroundings and the words of the wedding prayers—moved me to tears and filled me with triumph. I thought how my life had blossomed, how poetically it was shaping itself! Two years ago I was still a student, I was living in cheap furnished rooms, without money, without relations, and, as I fancied then, with nothing to look forward to. Now I am a teacher in the high school in one of the best provincial towns, with a secure income, loved, spoiled. It is for my sake, I thought, this crowd is collected, for my sake three candelabra have been lighted, the deacon is booming, the choir is doing its best; and it's for my sake that this young creature, whom I soon shall call my wife, is so young, so elegant, and so joyful. I recalled our first meetings, our rides into the country, my declaration of love and the weather, which, as though expressly, was so exquisitely fine all the summer; and the happiness which at one time in my old rooms seemed to me possible only in novels and stories, I was now experiencing in reality—I was now, as it were, holding it in my hands.

"After the ceremony they all crowded in disorder round Masha and me, expressed their genuine pleasure, congratulated us and wished us joy. The brigadier-general, an old man of seventy, confined himself to congratulating Masha, and said to her in a squeaky, aged voice, so loud that it could be heard all over the church:

"'I hope that even after you are married you may remain the rose you are now, my dear.'

"The officers, the director, and all the teachers smiled from politeness, and I was conscious of an agreeable artificial smile on my face, too. Dear Ippolit Ippolititch, the teacher of history and geography, who always says what every one has heard before, pressed my hand warmly and said with feeling:

"'Hitherto you have been unmarried and have lived alone, and now you are married and no longer single.'

"From the church we went to a two-storied house which I am receiving as part of the dowry. Besides that house Masha is bringing me twenty thousand roubles, as well as a piece of waste land with a shanty on it, where I am told there are numbers of hens and ducks which are not looked after and are turning wild. When I got home from the church, I stretched myself at full length on the low sofa in my new study and began to smoke; I felt snug, cosy, and comfortable, as I never had in my life before. And meanwhile the wedding party were shouting 'Hurrah!' while a wretched band in the hall played flourishes and all sorts of trash. Varya, Masha's sister, ran into the study with a wineglass in her hand, and with a queer, strained expression, as though her mouth were full of water; apparently she had meant to go on further, but she suddenly burst out laughing and sobbing, and the wineglass crashed on the floor. We took her by the arms and led her away.

"'Nobody can understand!' she muttered afterwards, lying on the old nurse's bed in a back room. 'Nobody, nobody! My God, nobody can understand!'

"But every one understood very well that she was four years older than her sister Masha, and still unmarried, and that she was crying, not from envy, but from the melancholy consciousness that her time was passing, and perhaps had passed. When they danced the quadrille, she was back in the drawing-room with a tear-stained and heavily powdered face, and I saw Captain Polyansky holding a plate of ice before her while she ate it with a spoon.

"It is past five o'clock in the morning. I took up my diary to describe my complete and perfect happiness, and thought I would write a good six pages, and read it tomorrow to Masha; but, strange to say, everything is muddled in my head and as misty as a dream, and I can remember vividly nothing but that episode with Varya, and I want to write, 'Poor Varya!' I could go on sitting here and writing 'Poor Varya!' By the way, the trees have begun rustling; it will rain. The crows are cawing, and my Masha, who has just gone to sleep, has for some reason a sorrowful face."

For a long while afterwards Nikitin did not write his diary. At the beginning of August he had the school examinations, and after the fifteenth the classes began. As a rule he set off for school before nine in the morning, and before ten o'clock he was looking at his watch and pining for his Masha and his new house. In the lower forms he would set some boy to dictate, and while the boys were writing, would sit in the window with his eyes shut, dreaming; whether he dreamed of the future or recalled the past, everything seemed to him equally delightful, like a fairy tale. In the senior classes they were reading aloud Gogol or Pushkin's prose works, and that made him sleepy; people, trees, fields, horses, rose before his imagination, and he would say with a sigh, as though fascinated by the author:

"How lovely!"

At the midday recess Masha used to send him lunch in a snow-white napkin, and he would eat it slowly, with pauses, to prolong the enjoyment of it; and Ippolit Ippolititch, whose lunch as a rule consisted of nothing but bread, looked at him with respect and envy, and gave expression to some familiar fact, such as:

"Men cannot live without food."

After school Nikitin went straight to give his private lessons, and when at last by six o'clock he got home, he felt excited and anxious, as though he had been away for a year. He would run upstairs breathless, find Masha, throw his arms round her, and kiss her and swear that he loved her, that he could not live without her, declare that he had missed her fearfully, and ask her in trepidation how she was and why she looked so depressed. Then they would dine together. After dinner he would lie on the sofa in his study and smoke, while she sat beside him and talked in a low voice.

His happiest days now were Sundays and holidays, when he was at home from morning till evening. On those days he took part in the naïve but extraordinarily pleasant life which reminded him of a pastoral idyl. He was never weary of watching how his sensible and practical Masha was arranging her nest, and anxious to show that he was of some use in the house, he would do something useless— for instance, bring the chaise out of the stable and look at it from every side. Masha had installed a regular dairy with three cows, and in her cellar she had many jugs of milk and pots of sour cream, and she kept it all for butter. Sometimes, by way of a joke, Nikitin would ask her for a glass of milk, and she would be quite upset because it was against her rules; but he would laugh and throw his arms round her, saying:

"There, there; I was joking, my darling! I was joking!"

Or he would laugh at her strictness when, finding in the cupboard some stale bit of cheese or sausage as hard as a stone, she would say seriously:

"They will eat that in the kitchen."

He would observe that such a scrap was only fit for a mousetrap, and she would reply warmly that men knew nothing about housekeeping, and that it was just the same to the servants if you were to send down a hundredweight of savouries to the kitchen. He would agree, and embrace her enthusiastically. Everything that was just in what she said seemed to him extraordinary and amazing; and what did not fit in with his convictions seemed to him naïve and touching.

Sometimes he was in a philosophical mood, and he would begin to discuss some abstract subject while she listened and looked at his face with curiosity.

"I am immensely happy with you, my joy," he used to say, playing with her fingers or plaiting and unplaiting her hair. "But I don't look upon this happiness of mine as something that has come to me by chance, as though it had dropped from heaven. This happiness is a perfectly natural, consistent, logical consequence. I believe that man is the creator of his own happiness, and now I am enjoying just what I have myself created. Yes, I speak without false modesty: I have created this happiness myself and I have a right to it. You know my past. My unhappy childhood, without father or mother; my depressing youth, poverty—all this was a struggle, all this was the path by which I made my way to happiness. . . ."

In October the school sustained a heavy loss: Ippolit Ippolititch was taken ill with erysipelas on the head and died. For two days before his death he was unconscious and delirious, but even in his delirium he said nothing that was not perfectly well known to every one.

"The Volga flows into the Caspian Sea. . . . Horses eat oats and hay. . . ."

There were no lessons at the high school on the day of his funeral. His colleagues and pupils were the coffin-bearers, and the school choir sang all the way to the grave the anthem "Holy God." Three priests, two deacons, all his pupils and the staff of the boys' high school, and the bishop's choir in their best kaftans, took part in the procession. And passers-by who met the solemn procession, crossed themselves and said:

"God grant us all such a death."

Returning home from the cemetery much moved, Nikitin got out his diary from the table and wrote:

"We have just consigned to the tomb Ippolit Ippolititch Ryzhitsky. Peace to your ashes, modest worker! Masha, Varya, and all the women at the funeral, wept from genuine feeling, perhaps because they knew this uninteresting, humble man had never been loved by a woman. I wanted to say a warm word at my colleague's grave, but I was warned that this might displease the director, as he did not like our poor friend. I believe that this is the first day since my marriage that my heart has been heavy."

There was no other event of note in the scholastic year.

The winter was mild, with wet snow and no frost; on Epiphany Eve, for instance, the wind howled all night as though it were autumn, and water trickled off the roofs; and in the morning, at the ceremony of the blessing of the water, the police allowed no one to go on the river, because they said the ice was swelling up and looked dark. But in spite of bad weather Nikitin's life was as happy as in summer. And, indeed, he acquired another source of pleasure; he learned to play vint. Only one thing troubled him, moved him to anger, and seemed to prevent him from being perfectly happy: the cats and dogs which formed part of his wife's dowry. The rooms, especially in the morning, always smelt like a menagerie, and nothing could destroy the odour; the cats frequently fought with the dogs. The spiteful beast Mushka was fed a dozen times a day; she still refused to recognize Nikitin and growled at him: "Rrr . . . nga-nga-nga!"

One night in Lent he was returning home from the club where he had been playing cards. It was dark, raining, and muddy. Nikitin had an unpleasant feeling at the bottom of his heart and could not account for it. He did not know whether it was because he had lost twelve roubles at cards, or whether because one of the players, when they were settling up, had said that of course Nikitin had pots of money, with obvious reference to his wife's portion. He did not regret the twelve roubles, and there was nothing offensive in what had been said; but, still, there was the unpleasant feeling. He did not even feel a desire to go home.

"Foo, how horrid!" he said, standing still at a lamp-post.

It occurred to him that he did not regret the twelve roubles because he got them for nothing. If he had been a working man he would have known the value of every farthing, and would not have been so careless whether he lost or won. And his good-fortune had all, he reflected, come to him by chance, for nothing, and really was as superfluous for him as medicine for the healthy. If, like the vast majority of people, he had been harassed by anxiety for his daily bread, had been struggling for existence, if his back and chest had ached from work, then supper, a warm snug home, and domestic happiness, would have been the necessity, the compensation, the crown of his life; as it was, all this had a strange, indefinite significance for him.

"Foo, how horrid!" he repeated, knowing perfectly well that these reflections were in themselves a bad sign.

When he got home Masha was in bed: she was breathing evenly and smiling, and was evidently sleeping with great enjoyment. Near her the white cat lay curled up, purring. While Nikitin lit the candle and lighted his cigarette, Masha woke up and greedily drank a glass of water.

"I ate too many sweets," she said, and laughed. "Have you been home?" she asked after a pause.

"No."

Nikitin knew already that Captain Polyansky, on whom Varya had been building great hopes of late, was being transferred to one of the western provinces, and was already making his farewell visits in the town, and so it was depressing at his father-in-law's.

"Varya looked in this evening," said Masha, sitting up. "She did not say anything, but one could see from her face how wretched she is, poor darling! I can't bear Polyansky. He is fat and bloated, and when he walks or dances his cheeks shake. . . . He is not a man I would choose. But, still, I did think he was a decent person."

"I think he is a decent person now," said Nikitin.

"Then why has he treated Varya so badly?"

"Why badly?" asked Nikitin, beginning to feel irritation against the white cat, who was stretching and arching its back. "As far as I know, he has made no proposal and has given her no promises."

"Then why was he so often at the house? If he didn't mean to marry her, he oughtn't to have come."

Nikitin put out the candle and got into bed. But he felt disinclined to lie down and to sleep. He felt as though his head were immense and empty as a barn, and that new, peculiar thoughts were wandering about in it like tall shadows. He thought that, apart from the soft light of the ikon lamp, that beamed upon their quiet domestic happiness, that apart from this little world in which he and this cat lived so peacefully and happily, there was another world. . . . And he had a passionate, poignant longing to be in that other world, to work himself at some factory or big workshop, to address big audiences, to write, to publish, to raise a stir, to exhaust himself, to suffer. . . . He wanted something that would engross him till he forgot himself, ceased to care for the personal happiness which yielded him only sensations so monotonous. And suddenly there rose vividly before his imagination the figure of Shebaldin with his clean-shaven face, saying to him with horror: "You haven't even read Lessing! You are quite behind the times! How you have gone to seed!"

Masha woke up and again drank some water. He glanced at her neck, at her plump shoulders and throat, and remembered the word the brigadier-general had used in church—"rose."

"Rose," he muttered, and laughed.

His laugh was answered by a sleepy growl from Mushka under the bed: "Rrr . . . nga-nga-nga . . . !"

A heavy anger sank like a cold weight on his heart, and he felt tempted to say something rude to Masha, and even to jump up and hit her; his heart began throbbing.

"So then," he asked, restraining himself, "since I went to your house, I was bound in duty to marry you?"

"Of course. You know that very well."

"That's nice." And a minute later he repeated: "That's nice."

To relieve the throbbing of his heart, and to avoid saying too much, Nikitin went to his study and lay down on the sofa, without a pillow; then he lay on the floor on the carpet.

"What nonsense it is!" he said to reassure himself. "You are a teacher, you are working in the noblest of callings. . . . What need have you of any other world? What rubbish!"

But almost immediately he told himself with conviction that he was not a real teacher, but simply a government employé, as commonplace and mediocre as the Czech who taught Greek. He had never had a vocation for teaching, he knew nothing of the theory of teaching, and never had been interested in the subject; he did not know how to treat children; he did not understand the significance of what he taught, and perhaps did not teach the right things. Poor Ippolit Ippolititch had been frankly stupid, and all the boys, as well as his colleagues, knew what he was and what to expect from him; but he, Nikitin, like the Czech, knew how to conceal his stupidity and cleverly deceived every one by pretending that, thank God, his teaching was a success. These new ideas frightened Nikitin; he rejected them, called them stupid, and believed that all this was due to his nerves, that he would laugh at himself.

And he did, in fact, by the morning laugh at himself and call himself an old woman; but it was clear to him that his peace of mind was lost, perhaps, for ever, and that in that little two-story house happiness was henceforth impossible for him. He realized that the illusion had evaporated, and that a new life of unrest and clear sight was beginning which was incompatible with peace and personal happiness.

Next day, which was Sunday, he was at the school chapel, and there met his colleagues and the director. It seemed to him that they were entirely preoccupied with concealing their ignorance and discontent with life, and he, too, to conceal his uneasiness, smiled affably and talked of trivialities. Then he went to the station and saw the mail train come in and go out, and it was agreeable to him to be alone and not to have to talk to any one.

At home he found Varya and his father-in-law, who had come to dinner. Varya's eyes were red with crying, and she complained of a headache, while Shelestov ate a great deal, saying that young men nowadays were unreliable, and that there was very little gentlemanly feeling among them.

"It's loutishness!" he said. "I shall tell him so to his face: 'It's loutishness, sir,' I shall say."

Nikitin smiled affably and helped Masha to look after their guests, but after dinner he went to his study and shut the door.

The March sun was shining brightly in at the windows and shedding its warm rays on the table. It was only the twentieth of the month, but already the cabmen were driving with wheels, and the starlings were noisy in the garden. It was just the weather in which Masha would come in, put one arm round his neck, tell him the horses were saddled or the chaise was at the door, and ask him what she should put on to keep warm. Spring was beginning as exquisitely as last spring, and it promised the same joys. . . . But Nikitin was thinking that it would be nice to take a holiday and go to Moscow, and stay at his old lodgings there. In the next room they were drinking coffee and talking of Captain Polyansky, while he tried not to listen and wrote in his diary: "Where am I, my God? I am surrounded by vulgarity and vulgarity. Wearisome, insignificant people, pots of sour cream, jugs of milk, cockroaches, stupid women. . . . There is nothing more terrible, mortifying, and distressing than vulgarity. I must escape from here, I must escape today, or I shall go out of my mind!"

NOTES

Count Nulin: Count Zero, after Pushkin's comic poem Count Nulin

Marie Godefroi: a famous circus bareback rider

Shtchedrin: M. E. Saltykov (1821-1889), satirist and novelist, used the pseudonym Shchedrin

Dostoevsky: Fyodor M. Dostoevsky (1821-1881), the famous novelist

Onyegin and then from Boris Godunov: Eugene Onegin, Pushkin's novel in verse; Boris Godunov was an historical play by Pushkin

The Woman who was a Sinner: a poem by Alexey K. Tolstoy (1817-1875); amateurs recited it so often it became a cliche and Chekhov later used the poem in his play The Cherry Orchard

Lessing: G. E. Lessing's 1769 treatise on drama was a central text in dramatic theory

"not for nothing...hussar": inexact quote from Lermontov

Battle of Kalka: 1223 battle in which the Russians were defeated by a Mongol-Tatar army

capes in Siberia: literally, "Cape Chukotskys," located opposite the Bering Straits

Vyestnik Evropi: European Herald, a liberal magazine

viva voce: oral exams

Gogol: Nikolay V. Gogol (1809-1852) Russian writer

blessing of the water: annual Russian Orthodox Church ceremony held on January 5

vint: a bridge-like card game

driving with wheels: as opposed to sleigh-runners in winter

NOT WANTED

Between six and seven o'clock on a July evening, a crowd of summer visitors—mostly fathers of families—burdened with parcels, portfolios, and ladies' hat-boxes, was trailing along from the little station of Helkovo, in the direction of the summer villas. They all looked exhausted, hungry, and ill-humoured, as though the sun were not shining and the grass were not green for them.

Trudging along among the others was Pavel Matveyitch Zaikin, a member of the Circuit Court, a tall, stooping man, in a cheap cotton dust-coat and with a cockade on his faded cap. He was perspiring, red in the face, and gloomy. . . .

"Do you come out to your holiday home every day?" said a summer visitor, in ginger-coloured trousers, addressing him.

"No, not every day," Zaikin answered sullenly. "My wife and son are staying here all the while, and I come down two or three times a week. I haven't time to come every day; besides, it is expensive."

"You're right there; it is expensive," sighed he of the ginger trousers. "In town you can't walk to the station, you have to take a cab; and then, the ticket costs forty-two kopecks; you buy a paper for the journey; one is tempted to drink a glass of vodka. It's all petty expenditure not worth considering, but, mind you, in the course of the summer it will run up to some two hundred roubles. Of course, to be in the lap of Nature is worth any money—I don't dispute it . . . idyllic and all the rest of it; but of course, with the salary an official gets, as you know yourself, every farthing has to be considered. If you waste a halfpenny you lie awake all night. . . . Yes. . . I receive, my dear sir—I haven't the honour of knowing your name—I receive a salary of very nearly two thousand roubles a year. I am a civil councillor, I smoke second-rate tobacco, and I haven't a rouble to spare to buy Vichy water, prescribed me by the doctor for gall-stones."

"It's altogether abominable," said Zaikin after a brief silence. "I maintain, sir, that summer holidays are the invention of the devil and of woman. The devil was actuated in the present instance by malice, woman by excessive frivolity. Mercy on us, it is not life at all; it is hard labour, it is hell! It's hot and stifling, you can hardly breathe, and you wander about like a lost soul and can find no refuge. In town there is no furniture, no servants. . . everything has been carried off to the villa: you eat what you can get; you go without your tea because there is no one to heat the samovar; you can't wash yourself; and when you come down here into this 'lap of Nature' you have to walk, if you please, through the dust and heat. . . . Phew! Are you married?"

"Yes. . . three children," sighs Ginger Trousers.

"It's abominable altogether. . . . It's a wonder we are still alive."

At last the summer visitors reached their destination. Zaikin said good-bye to Ginger Trousers and went into his villa. He found a death-like silence in the house. He could hear nothing but the buzzing of the gnats, and the prayer for help of a fly destined for the dinner of a spider. The windows were hung with muslin curtains, through which the faded flowers of the geraniums showed red. On the unpainted wooden walls near the oleographs flies were slumbering. There was not a soul in the passage, the kitchen, or the dining-room. In the room which was called indifferently the parlour or the drawing-room, Zaikin found his son Petya, a little boy of six. Petya was sitting at the table, and breathing loudly with his lower lip stuck out, was engaged in cutting out the figure of a knave of diamonds from a card.

"Oh, that's you, father!" he said, without turning round. "Good-evening."

"Good-evening. . . . And where is mother?"

"Mother? She is gone with Olga Kirillovna to a rehearsal of the play. The day after tomorrow they will have a performance. And they will take me, too. . . . And will you go?"

"H'm! . . . When is she coming back?"

"She said she would be back in the evening."

"And where is Natalya?"

"Mamma took Natalya with her to help her dress for the performance, and Akulina has gone to the wood to get mushrooms. Father, why is it that when gnats bite you their stomachs get red?"

"I don't know. . . . Because they suck blood. So there is no one in the house, then?"

"No one; I am all alone in the house."

Zaikin sat down in an easy-chair, and for a moment gazed blankly at the window.

"Who is going to get our dinner?" he asked.

"They haven't cooked any dinner today, father. Mamma thought you were not coming today, and did not order any dinner. She is going to have dinner with Olga Kirillovna at the rehearsal."

"Oh, thank you very much; and you, what have you to eat?"

"I've had some milk. They bought me six kopecks' worth of milk. And, father, why do gnats suck blood?"

Zaikin suddenly felt as though something heavy were rolling down on his liver and beginning to gnaw it. He felt so vexed, so aggrieved, and so bitter, that he was choking and tremulous; he wanted to jump up, to bang something on the floor, and to burst into loud abuse; but then he remembered that his doctor had absolutely forbidden him all excitement, so he got up, and making an effort to control himself, began whistling a tune from "Les Huguenots."

"Father, can you act in plays?" he heard Petya's voice.

"Oh, don't worry me with stupid questions!" said Zaikin, getting angry. "He sticks to one like a leaf in the bath! Here you are, six years old, and just as silly as you were three years ago. . . . Stupid, neglected child! Why are you spoiling those cards, for instance? How dare you spoil them?"

"These cards aren't yours," said Petya, turning round. "Natalya gave them me."

"You are telling fibs, you are telling fibs, you horrid boy!" said Zaikin, growing more and more irritated. "You are always telling fibs! You want a whipping, you horrid little pig! I will pull your ears!"

Petya leapt up, and craning his neck, stared fixedly at his father's red and wrathful face. His big eyes first began blinking, then were dimmed with moisture, and the boy's face began working.

"But why are you scolding?" squealed Petya. "Why do you attack me, you stupid? I am not interfering with anybody; I am not naughty; I do what I am told, and yet . . . you are cross! Why are you scolding me?"

The boy spoke with conviction, and wept so bitterly that Zaikin felt conscience-stricken.

"Yes, really, why am I falling foul of him?" he thought. "Come, come," he said, touching the boy on the shoulder. "I am sorry, Petya . . . forgive me. You are my good boy, my nice boy, I love you."

Petya wiped his eyes with his sleeve, sat down, with a sigh, in the same place and began cutting out the queen. Zaikin went off to his own room. He stretched himself on the sofa, and putting his hands behind his head, sank into thought. The boy's tears had softened his anger, and by degrees the oppression on his liver grew less. He felt nothing but exhaustion and hunger.

"Father," he heard on the other side of the door, "shall I show you my collection of insects?"

"Yes, show me."

Petya came into the study and handed his father a long green box. Before raising it to his ear Zaikin could hear a despairing buzz and the scratching of claws on the sides of the box. Opening the lid, he saw a number of butterflies, beetles, grasshoppers, and flies fastened to the bottom of the box with pins. All except two or three butterflies were still alive and moving.

"Why, the grasshopper is still alive!" said Petya in surprise. "I caught him yesterday morning, and he is still alive!"

"Who taught you to pin them in this way?"

"Olga Kirillovna."

"Olga Kirillovna ought to be pinned down like that herself!" said Zaikin with repulsion. "Take them away! It's shameful to torture animals."

"My God! How horribly he is being brought up!" he thought, as Petya went out.

Pavel Matveyitch forgot his exhaustion and hunger, and thought of nothing but his boy's future. Meanwhile, outside the light was gradually fading. . . . He could hear the summer visitors trooping back from the evening bathe. Some one was stopping near the open dining-room window and shouting: "Do you want any mushrooms?" And getting no answer, shuffled on with bare feet. . . . But at last, when the dusk was so thick that the outlines of the geraniums behind the muslin curtain were lost, and whiffs of the freshness of evening were coming in at the window, the door of the passage was thrown open noisily, and there came a sound of rapid footsteps, talk, and laughter. . . .

"Mamma!" shrieked Petya.

Zaikin peeped out of his study and saw his wife, Nadyezhda Stepanovna, healthy and rosy as ever; with her he saw Olga Kirillovna, a spare woman with fair hair and heavy freckles, and two unknown men: one a lanky young man with curly red hair and a big Adam's apple; the other, a short stubby man with a shaven face like an actor's and a bluish crooked chin.

"Natalya, set the samovar," cried Nadyezhda Stepanovna, with a loud rustle of her skirts. "I hear Pavel Matveyitch is come. Pavel, where are you? Good-evening, Pavel!" she said, running into the study breathlessly. "So you've come. I am so glad. . . . Two of our amateurs have come with me. . . . Come, I'll introduce you. . . . Here, the taller one is Koromyslov . . . he sings splendidly; and the other, the little one . . . is called Smerkalov: he is a real actor . . . he recites magnificently. Oh, how tired I am! We have just had a rehearsal. . . . It goes splendidly. We are acting 'The Lodger with the Trombone' and 'Waiting for Him.' . . . The performance is the day after tomorrow. . . ."

"Why did you bring them?" asked Zaikin.

"I couldn't help it, Poppet; after tea we must rehearse our parts and sing something. . . . I am to sing a duet with Koromyslov. . . . Oh, yes, I was almost forgetting! Darling, send Natalya to get some sardines, vodka, cheese, and something else. They will most likely stay to supper. . . . Oh, how tired I am!"

"H'm! I've no money."

"You must, Poppet! It would be awkward! Don't make me blush."

Half an hour later Natalya was sent for vodka and savouries; Zaikin, after drinking tea and eating a whole French loaf, went to his bedroom and lay down on the bed, while Nadyezhda Stepanovna and her visitors, with much noise and laughter, set to work to rehearse their parts. For a long time Pavel Matveyitch heard Koromyslov's nasal reciting and Smerkalov's theatrical exclamations. . . . The rehearsal was followed by a long conversation, interrupted by the shrill laughter of Olga Kirillovna. Smerkalov, as a real actor, explained the parts with aplomb and heat. . . .

Then followed the duet, and after the duet there was the clatter of crockery. . . . Through his drowsiness Zaikin heard them persuading Smerkalov to read "The Woman who was a Sinner," and heard him, after affecting to refuse, begin to recite. He hissed, beat himself on the breast, wept, laughed in a husky bass. . . . Zaikin scowled and hid his head under the quilt.

"It's a long way for you to go, and it's dark," he heard Nadyezhda Stepanovna's voice an hour later. "Why shouldn't you stay the night here? Koromyslov can sleep here in the drawing-room on the sofa, and you, Smerkalov, in Petya's bed. . . . I can put Petya in my husband's study. . . . Do stay, really!"

At last when the clock was striking two, all was hushed, the bedroom door opened, and Nadyezhda Stepanovna appeared.

"Pavel, are you asleep?" she whispered.

"No; why?"

"Go into your study, darling, and lie on the sofa. I am going to put Olga Kirillovna here, in your bed. Do go, dear! I would put her to sleep in the study, but she is afraid to sleep alone. . . . Do get up!"

Zaikin got up, threw on his dressing-gown, and taking his pillow, crept wearily to the study. . . . Feeling his way to his sofa, he lighted a match, and saw Petya lying on the sofa. The boy was not asleep, and, looking at the match with wide-open eyes:

"Father, why is it gnats don't go to sleep at night?" he asked.

"Because . . . because . . . you and I are not wanted. . . . We have nowhere to sleep even."

"Father, and why is it Olga Kirillovna has freckles on her face?"

"Oh, shut up! I am tired of you."

After a moment's thought, Zaikin dressed and went out into the street for a breath of air. . . . He looked at the grey morning sky, at the motionless clouds, heard the lazy call of the drowsy corncrake, and began dreaming of the next day, when he would go to town, and coming back from the court would tumble into bed. . . . Suddenly the figure of a man appeared round the corner.

"A watchman, no doubt," thought Zaikin. But going nearer and looking more closely he recognized in the figure the summer visitor in the ginger trousers.

"You're not asleep?" he asked.

"No, I can't sleep," sighed Ginger Trousers. "I am enjoying Nature . . . . A welcome visitor, my wife's mother, arrived by the night train, you know. She brought with her our nieces . . . splendid girls! I was delighted to see them, although . . . it's very damp! And you, too, are enjoying Nature?"

"Yes," grunted Zaikin, "I am enjoying it, too. . . . Do you know whether there is any sort of tavern or restaurant in the neighbourhood?"

Ginger Trousers raised his eyes to heaven and meditated profoundly.

NOTES

villa: "dacha," a summer residence

I am a civil councillor: Rank 5 in the Civil Service; entitled to be called "Your Excellency"

Vichy water: an effervescent mineral water

oleographs: imitation oil paintings

Les Huguenots: 1835 opera by Jacob Meyerbeer (1791-1864)

Poppet: a term of endearment

"The Woman who was a Sinner": a poem by Aleksey Tolstoy (1817-1875)

TYPHUS

A young lieutenant called Klimov was travelling from Petersburg to Moscow in a smoking carriage of the mail train. Opposite him was sitting an elderly man with a shaven face like a sea captain's, by all appearances a well-to-do Finn or Swede. He pulled at his pipe the whole journey and kept talking about the same subject:

"Ha, you are an officer! I have a brother an officer too, only he is a naval officer. . . . He is a naval officer, and he is stationed at Kronstadt. Why are you going to Moscow?"

"I am serving there."

"Ha! And are you a family man?"

"No, I live with my sister and aunt."

"My brother's an officer, only he is a naval officer; he has a wife and three children. Ha!"

The Finn seemed continually surprised at something, and gave a broad idiotic grin when he exclaimed "Ha!" and continually puffed at his stinking pipe. Klimov, who for some reason did not feel well, and found it burdensome to answer questions, hated him with all his heart. He dreamed of how nice it would be to snatch the wheezing pipe out of his hand and fling it under the seat, and drive the Finn himself into another compartment.

"Detestable people these Finns and . . . Greeks," he thought. "Absolutely superfluous, useless, detestable people. They simply fill up space on the earthly globe. What are they for?"

And the thought of Finns and Greeks produced a feeling akin to sickness all over his body. For the sake of comparison he tried to think of the French, of the Italians, but his efforts to think of these people evoked in his mind, for some reason, nothing but images of organ-grinders, naked women, and the foreign oleographs which hung over the chest of drawers at home, at his aunt's.

Altogether the officer felt in an abnormal state. He could not arrange his arms and legs comfortably on the seat, though he had the whole seat to himself. His mouth felt dry and sticky; there was a heavy fog in his brain; his thoughts seemed to be straying, not only within his head, but outside his skull, among the seats and the people that were shrouded in the darkness of night. Through the mist in his brain, as through a dream, he heard the murmur of voices, the rumble of wheels, the slamming of doors. The sounds of the bells, the whistles, the guards, the running to and fro of passengers on the platforms, seemed more frequent than usual. The time flew by rapidly, imperceptibly, and so it seemed as though the train were stopping at stations every minute, and metallic voices crying continually:

"Is the mail ready?"

"Yes!" was repeatedly coming from outside.

It seemed as though the man in charge of the heating came in too often to look at the thermometer, that the noise of trains going in the opposite direction and the rumble of the wheels over the bridges was incessant. The noise, the whistles, the Finn, the tobacco smoke—all this mingling with the menace and flickering of the misty images in his brain, the shape and character of which a man in health can never recall, weighed upon Klimov like an unbearable nightmare. In horrible misery he lifted his heavy head, looked at the lamp in the rays of which shadows and misty blurs seemed to be dancing. He wanted to ask for water, but his parched tongue would hardly move, and he scarcely had strength to answer the Finn's questions. He tried to lie down more comfortably and go to sleep, but he could not succeed. The Finn several times fell asleep, woke up again, lighted his pipe, addressed him with his "Ha!" and went to sleep again; and still the lieutenant's legs could not get into a comfortable position, and still the menacing images stood facing him.

At Spirovo he went out into the station for a drink of water. He saw people sitting at the table and hurriedly eating.

"And how can they eat!" he thought, trying not to sniff the air, that smelt of roast meat, and not to look at the munching mouths — they both seemed to him sickeningly disgusting.

A good-looking lady was conversing loudly with a military man in a red cap, and showing magnificent white teeth as she smiled; and the smile, and the teeth, and the lady herself made on Klimov the same revolting impression as the ham and the rissoles. He could not understand how it was the military man in the red cap was not ill at ease, sitting beside her and looking at her healthy, smiling face.

When after drinking some water he went back to his carriage, the Finn was sitting smoking; his pipe was wheezing and squelching like a golosh with holes in it in wet weather.

"Ha!" he said, surprised; "what station is this?"

"I don't know," answered Klimov, lying down and shutting his mouth that he might not breathe the acrid tobacco smoke.

"And when shall we reach Tver?"

"I don't know. Excuse me, I . . . I can't answer. I am ill. I caught cold today."

The Finn knocked his pipe against the window-frame and began talking of his brother, the naval officer. Klimov no longer heard him; he was thinking miserably of his soft, comfortable bed, of a bottle of cold water, of his sister Katya, who was so good at making one comfortable, soothing, giving one water. He even smiled when the vision of his orderly Pavel, taking off his heavy stifling boots and putting water on the little table, flitted through his imagination. He fancied that if he could only get into his bed, have a drink of water, his nightmare would give place to sound healthy sleep.

"Is the mail ready?" a hollow voice reached him from the distance.

"Yes," answered a bass voice almost at the window.

It was already the second or third station from Spirovo.

The time was flying rapidly in leaps and bounds, and it seemed as though the bells, whistles, and stoppings would never end. In despair Klimov buried his face in the corner of the seat, clutched his head in his hands, and began again thinking of his sister Katya and his orderly Pavel, but his sister and his orderly were mixed up with the misty images in his brain, whirled round, and disappeared. His burning breath, reflected from the back of the seat, seemed to scald his face; his legs were uncomfortable; there was a draught from the window on his back; but, however wretched he was, he did not want to change his position. . . . A heavy nightmarish lethargy gradually gained possession of him and fettered his limbs.

When he brought himself to raise his head, it was already light in the carriage. The passengers were putting on their fur coats and moving about. The train was stopping. Porters in white aprons and with discs on their breasts were bustling among the passengers and snatching up their boxes. Klimov put on his great-coat, mechanically followed the other passengers out of the carriage, and it seemed to him that not he, but some one else was moving, and he felt that his fever, his thirst, and the menacing images which had not let him sleep all night, came out of the carriage with him. Mechanically he took his luggage and engaged a sledge-driver. The man asked him for a rouble and a quarter to drive to Povarsky Street, but he did not haggle, and without protest got submissively into the sledge. He still understood the difference of numbers, but money had ceased to have any value to him.

At home Klimov was met by his aunt and his sister Katya, a girl of eighteen. When Katya greeted him she had a pencil and exercise book in her hand, and he remembered that she was preparing for an examination as a teacher. Gasping with fever, he walked aimlessly through all the rooms without answering their questions or greetings, and when he reached his bed he sank down on the pillow. The Finn, the red cap, the lady with the white teeth, the smell of roast meat, the flickering blurs, filled his consciousness, and by now he did not know where he was and did not hear the agitated voices.

When he recovered consciousness he found himself in bed, undressed, saw a bottle of water and Pavel, but it was no cooler, nor softer, nor more comfortable for that. His arms and legs, as before, refused to lie comfortably; his tongue stuck to the roof of his mouth, and he heard the wheezing of the Finn's pipe. . . . A stalwart, black-bearded doctor was busy doing something beside the bed, brushing against Pavel with his broad back.

"It's all right, it's all right, young man," he muttered. "Excellent, excellent . . . goo-od, goo-od . . . !"

The doctor called Klimov "young man," said "goo-od" instead of "good" and "so-o" instead of "so."

"So-o . . . so-o . . . so-o," he murmured. "Goo-od, goo-od . . . ! Excellent, young man. You mustn't lose heart!"

The doctor's rapid, careless talk, his well-fed countenance, and condescending "young man," irritated Klimov.

"Why do you call me 'young man'?" he moaned. "What familiarity! Damn it all!"

And he was frightened by his own voice. The voice was so dried up, so weak and peevish, that he would not have known it.

"Excellent, excellent!" muttered the doctor, not in the least offended. . . . "You mustn't get angry, so-o, so-o, so-s. . . ."

And the time flew by at home with the same startling swiftness as in the railway carriage. The daylight was continually being replaced by the dusk of evening. The doctor seemed never to leave his bedside, and he heard at every moment his "so-o, so-o, so-o." A continual succession of people was incessantly crossing the bedroom. Among them were: Pavel, the Finn, Captain Yaroshevitch, Lance-Corporal Maximenko, the red cap, the lady with the white teeth, the doctor. They were all talking and waving their arms, smoking and eating. Once by daylight Klimov saw the chaplain of the regiment, Father

Alexandr, who was standing before the bed, wearing a stole and with a prayer-book in his hand. He was muttering something with a grave face such as Klimov had never seen in him before. The lieutenant remembered that Father Alexandr used in a friendly way to call all the Catholic officers "Poles," and wanting to amuse him, he cried:

"Father, Yaroshevitch the Pole has climbed up a pole!"

But Father Alexandr, a light-hearted man who loved a joke, did not smile, but became graver than ever, and made the sign of the cross over Klimov. At night-time by turn two shadows came noiselessly in and out; they were his aunt and sister. His sister's shadow knelt down and prayed; she bowed down to the ikon, and her grey shadow on the wall bowed down too, so that two shadows were praying. The whole time there was a smell of roast meat and the Finn's pipe, but once Klimov smelt the strong smell of incense. He felt so sick he could not lie still, and began shouting:

"The incense! Take away the incense!"

There was no answer. He could only hear the subdued singing of the priest somewhere and some one running upstairs.

When Klimov came to himself there was not a soul in his bedroom. The morning sun was streaming in at the window through the lower blind, and a quivering sunbeam, bright and keen as the sword's edge, was flashing on the glass bottle. He heard the rattle of wheels—so there was no snow now in the street. The lieutenant looked at the ray, at the familiar furniture, at the door, and the first thing he did was to laugh. His chest and stomach heaved with delicious, happy, tickling laughter. His whole body from head to foot was overcome by a sensation of infinite happiness and joy in life, such as the first man must have felt when he was created and first saw the world. Klimov felt a passionate desire for movement, people, talk. His body lay a motionless block; only his hands stirred, but that he hardly noticed, and his whole attention was concentrated on trifles. He rejoiced in his breathing, in his laughter, rejoiced in the existence of the water-bottle, the ceiling, the sunshine, the tape on the curtains. God's world, even in the narrow space of his bedroom, seemed beautiful, varied, grand. When the doctor made his appearance, the lieutenant was thinking what a delicious thing medicine was, how charming and pleasant the doctor was, and how nice and interesting people were in general.

"So-o, so, so. . . Excellent, excellent! . . . Now we are well again. . . . Goo-od, goo-od!" the doctor pattered.

The lieutenant listened and laughed joyously; he remembered the

Finn, the lady with the white teeth, the train, and he longed to smoke, to eat.

"Doctor," he said, "tell them to give me a crust of rye bread and salt, and . . . and sardines."

The doctor refused; Pavel did not obey the order, and did not go for the bread. The lieutenant could not bear this and began crying like a naughty child.

"Baby!" laughed the doctor. "Mammy, bye-bye!"

Klimov laughed, too, and when the doctor went away he fell into a sound sleep. He woke up with the same joyfulness and sensation of happiness. His aunt was sitting near the bed.

"Well, aunt," he said joyfully. "What has been the matter?"

"Spotted typhus."

"Really. But now I am well, quite well! Where is Katya?"

"She is not at home. I suppose she has gone somewhere from her examination."

The old lady said this and looked at her stocking; her lips began quivering, she turned away, and suddenly broke into sobs. Forgetting the doctor's prohibition in her despair, she said:

"Ah, Katya, Katya! Our angel is gone! Is gone!"

She dropped her stocking and bent down to it, and as she did so her cap fell off her head. Looking at her grey head and understanding nothing, Klimov was frightened for Katya, and asked:

"Where is she, aunt?"

The old woman, who had forgotten Klimov and was thinking only of her sorrow, said:

"She caught typhus from you, and is dead. She was buried the day before yesterday."

This terrible, unexpected news was fully grasped by Klimov's consciousness; but terrible and startling as it was, it could not overcome the animal joy that filled the convalescent. He cried and laughed, and soon began scolding because they would not let him eat.

Only a week later when, leaning on Pavel, he went in his dressing-gown to the window, looked at the overcast spring sky and listened to the unpleasant clang of the old iron rails which were being carted by, his heart ached, he burst into tears, and leaned his forehead against the window-frame.

"How miserable I am!" he muttered. "My God, how miserable!"

And joy gave way to the boredom of everyday life and the feeling of his irrevocable loss.

A MISFORTUNE

Sofya Petrovna, the wife of Lubyantsev the notary, a handsome young woman of five-and-twenty, was walking slowly along a track that had been cleared in the wood, with Ilyin, a lawyer who was spending the summer in the neighbourhood. It was five o'clock in the evening. Feathery-white masses of cloud stood overhead; patches of bright blue sky peeped out between them. The clouds stood motionless, as though they had caught in the tops of the tall old pine-trees. It was still and sultry.

Farther on, the track was crossed by a low railway embankment on which a sentinel with a gun was for some reason pacing up and down. Just beyond the embankment there was a large white church with six domes and a rusty roof.

"I did not expect to meet you here," said Sofya Petrovna, looking at the ground and prodding at the last year's leaves with the tip of her parasol, "and now I am glad we have met. I want to speak to you seriously and once for all. I beg you, Ivan Mihalovitch, if you really love and respect me, please make an end of this pursuit of me! You follow me about like a shadow, you are continually looking at me not in a nice way, making love to me, writing me strange letters, and . . . and I don't know where it's all going to end! Why, what can come of it?"

Ilyin said nothing. Sofya Petrovna walked on a few steps and continued:

"And this complete transformation in you all came about in the course of two or three weeks, after five years' friendship. I don't know you, Ivan Mihalovitch!"

Sofya Petrovna stole a glance at her companion. Screwing up his eyes, he was looking intently at the fluffy clouds. His face looked angry, ill-humoured, and preoccupied, like that of a man in pain forced to listen to nonsense.

"I wonder you don't see it yourself," Madame Lubyantsev went on, shrugging her shoulders. "You ought to realize that it's not a very nice part you are playing. I am married; I love and respect my husband. . . . I have a daughter . . . . Can you think all that means nothing? Besides, as an old friend you know my attitude to family life and my views as to the sanctity of marriage."

Ilyin cleared his throat angrily and heaved a sigh.

"Sanctity of marriage . . ." he muttered. "Oh, Lord!"

"Yes, yes. . . . I love my husband, I respect him; and in any case I value the peace of my home. I would rather let myself be killed than be a cause of unhappiness to Andrey and his daughter. . . . And I beg you, Ivan Mihalovitch, for God's sake, leave me in peace! Let us be as good, true friends as we used to be, and give up these sighs and groans, which really don't suit you. It's settled and over! Not a word more about it. Let us talk of something else."

Sofya Petrovna again stole a glance at Ilyin's face. Ilyin was looking up; he was pale, and was angrily biting his quivering lips. She could not understand why he was angry and why he was indignant, but his pallor touched her.

"Don't be angry; let us be friends," she said affectionately. "Agreed? Here's my hand."

Ilyin took her plump little hand in both of his, squeezed it, and slowly raised it to his lips.

"I am not a schoolboy," he muttered. "I am not in the least tempted by friendship with the woman I love."

"Enough, enough! It's settled and done with. We have reached the seat; let us sit down."

Sofya Petrovna's soul was filled with a sweet sense of relief: the most difficult and delicate thing had been said, the painful question was settled and done with. Now she could breathe freely and look Ilyin straight in the face. She looked at him, and the egoistic feeling of the superiority of the woman over the man who loves her, agreeably flattered her. It pleased her to see this huge, strong man, with his manly, angry face and his big black beard—clever, cultivated, and, people said, talented—sit down obediently beside her and bow his head dejectedly. For two or three minutes they sat without speaking.

"Nothing is settled or done with," began Ilyin. "You repeat copybook maxims to me. 'I love and respect my husband . . . the sanctity of marriage. . . .' I know all that without your help, and I could tell you more, too. I tell you truthfully and honestly that I consider the way I am behaving as criminal and immoral. What more can one say than that? But what's the good of saying what everybody knows? Instead of feeding nightingales with paltry words, you had much better tell me what I am to do."

"I've told you already—go away."

"As you know perfectly well, I have gone away five times, and every time I turned back on the way. I can show you my through tickets —I've kept them all. I have not will enough to run away from you! I am struggling. I am struggling horribly; but what the devil am I good for if I have no backbone, if I am weak, cowardly! I can't struggle with Nature! Do you understand? I cannot! I run away from here, and she holds on to me and pulls me back. Contemptible, loathsome weakness!"

Ilyin flushed crimson, got up, and walked up and down by the seat.

"I feel as cross as a dog," he muttered, clenching his fists. "I hate and despise myself! My God! like some depraved schoolboy, I am making love to another man's wife, writing idiotic letters, degrading myself . . . ugh!"

Ilyin clutched at his head, grunted, and sat down. "And then your insincerity!" he went on bitterly. "If you do dislike my disgusting behaviour, why have you come here? What drew you here? In my letters I only ask you for a direct, definite answer—yes or no; but instead of a direct answer, you contrive every day these 'chance' meetings with me and regale me with copy-book maxims!"

Madame Lubyantsev was frightened and flushed. She suddenly felt the awkwardness which a decent woman feels when she is accidentally discovered undressed.

"You seem to suspect I am playing with you," she muttered. "I have always given you a direct answer, and . . . only today I've begged you . . ."

"Ough! as though one begged in such cases! If you were to say straight out 'Get away,' I should have been gone long ago; but you've never said that. You've never once given me a direct answer. Strange indecision! Yes, indeed; either you are playing with me, or else . . ."

Ilyin leaned his head on his fists without finishing. Sofya Petrovna began going over in her own mind the way she had behaved from beginning to end. She remembered that not only in her actions, but even in her secret thoughts, she had always been opposed to Ilyin's love-making; but yet she felt there was a grain of truth in the lawyer's words. But not knowing exactly what the truth was, she could not find answers to make to Ilyin's complaint, however hard she thought. It was awkward to be silent, and, shrugging her shoulders, she said:

So I am to blame, it appears."

"I don't blame you for your insincerity," sighed Ilyin. "I did not mean that when I spoke of it. . . . Your insincerity is natural and in the order of things. If people agreed together and suddenly became sincere, everything would go to the devil."

Sofya Petrovna was in no mood for philosophical reflections, but she was glad of a chance to change the conversation, and asked:

"But why?"

"Because only savage women and animals are sincere. Once civilization has introduced a demand for such comforts as, for instance, feminine virtue, sincerity is out of place. . . ."

Ilyin jabbed his stick angrily into the sand. Madame Lubyantsev listened to him and liked his conversation, though a great deal of it she did not understand. What gratified her most was that she, an ordinary woman, was talked to by a talented man on "intellectual" subjects; it afforded her great pleasure, too, to watch the working of his mobile, young face, which was still pale and angry. She failed to understand a great deal that he said, but what was clear to her in his words was the attractive boldness with which the modern man without hesitation or doubt decides great questions and draws conclusive deductions.

She suddenly realized that she was admiring him, and was alarmed.

"Forgive me, but I don't understand," she said hurriedly. "What makes you talk of insincerity? I repeat my request again: be my good, true friend; let me alone! I beg you most earnestly!"

"Very good; I'll try again," sighed Ilyin. "Glad to do my best. . . . Only I doubt whether anything will come of my efforts. Either I shall put a bullet through my brains or take to drink in an idiotic way. I shall come to a bad end! There's a limit to everything— to struggles with Nature, too. Tell me, how can one struggle against madness? If you drink wine, how are you to struggle against intoxication? What am I to do if your image has grown into my soul, and day and night stands persistently before my eyes, like that pine there at this moment? Come, tell me, what hard and difficult thing can I do to get free from this abominable, miserable condition, in which all my thoughts, desires, and dreams are no longer my own, but belong to some demon who has taken possession of me? I love you, love you so much that I am completely thrown out of gear; I've given up my work and all who are dear to me; I've forgotten my God! I've never been in love like this in my life."

Sofya Petrovna, who had not expected such a turn to their conversation, drew away from Ilyin and looked into his face in dismay.

Tears came into his eyes, his lips were quivering, and there was an imploring, hungry expression in his face.

"I love you!" he muttered, bringing his eyes near her big, frightened eyes. "You are so beautiful! I am in agony now, but I swear I would sit here all my life, suffering and looking in your eyes. But . . . be silent, I implore you!"

Sofya Petrovna, feeling utterly disconcerted, tried to think as quickly as possible of something to say to stop him. "I'll go away," she decided, but before she had time to make a movement to get up, Ilyin was on his knees before her. . . . He was clasping her knees, gazing into her face and speaking passionately, hotly, eloquently. In her terror and confusion she did not hear his words; for some reason now, at this dangerous moment, while her knees were being agreeably squeezed and felt as though they were in a warm bath, she was trying, with a sort of angry spite, to interpret her own sensations. She was angry that instead of brimming over with protesting virtue, she was entirely overwhelmed with weakness, apathy, and emptiness, like a drunken man utterly reckless; only at the bottom of her soul a remote bit of herself was malignantly taunting her: "Why don't you go? Is this as it should be? Yes?"

Seeking for some explanation, she could not understand how it was she did not pull away the hand to which Ilyin was clinging like a leech, and why, like Ilyin, she hastily glanced to right and to left to see whether any one was looking. The clouds and the pines stood motionless, looking at them severely, like old ushers seeing mischief, but bribed not to tell the school authorities. The sentry stood like a post on the embankment and seemed to be looking at the seat.

"Let him look," thought Sofya Petrovna.

"But . . . but listen," she said at last, with despair in her voice. "What can come of this? What will be the end of this?"

"I don't know, I don't know," he whispered, waving off the disagreeable questions.

They heard the hoarse, discordant whistle of the train. This cold, irrelevant sound from the everyday world of prose made Sofya Petrovna rouse herself.

"I can't stay . . . it's time I was at home," she said, getting up quickly. "The train is coming in. . . Andrey is coming by it! He will want his dinner."

Sofya Petrovna turned towards the embankment with a burning face. The engine slowly crawled by, then came the carriages. It was not the local train, as she had supposed, but a goods train. The trucks filed by against the background of the white church in a long string like the days of a man's life, and it seemed as though it would never end.

But at last the train passed, and the last carriage with the guard and a light in it had disappeared behind the trees. Sofya Petrovna turned round sharply, and without looking at Ilyin, walked rapidly back along the track. She had regained her self-possession. Crimson with shame, humiliated not by Ilyin—no, but by her own cowardice, by the shamelessness with which she, a chaste and high-principled woman, had allowed a man, not her husband, to hug her knees—she had only one thought now: to get home as quickly as possible to her villa, to her family. The lawyer could hardly keep pace with her. Turning from the clearing into a narrow path, she turned round and glanced at him so quickly that she saw nothing but the sand on his knees, and waved to him to drop behind.

Reaching home, Sofya Petrovna stood in the middle of her room for five minutes without moving, and looked first at the window and then at her writing-table.

"You low creature!" she said, upbraiding herself. "You low creature!"

To spite herself, she recalled in precise detail, keeping nothing back—she recalled that though all this time she had been opposed to Ilyin's lovemaking, something had impelled her to seek an interview with him; and what was more, when he was at her feet she had enjoyed it enormously. She recalled it all without sparing herself, and now, breathless with shame, she would have liked to slap herself in the face.

"Poor Andrey!" she said to herself, trying as she thought of her husband to put into her face as tender an expression as she could. "Varya, my poor little girl, doesn't know what a mother she has! Forgive me, my dear ones! I love you so much . . . so much!"

And anxious to prove to herself that she was still a good wife and mother, and that corruption had not yet touched that "sanctity of marriage" of which she had spoken to Ilyin, Sofya Petrovna ran to the kitchen and abused the cook for not having yet laid the table for Andrey Ilyitch. She tried to picture her husband's hungry and exhausted appearance, commiserated him aloud, and laid the table for him with her own hands, which she had never done before. Then she found her daughter Varya, picked her up in her arms and hugged her warmly; the child seemed to her cold and heavy, but she was unwilling to acknowledge this to herself, and she began explaining to the child how good, kind, and honourable her papa was.

But when Andrey Ilyitch arrived soon afterwards she hardly greeted him. The rush of false feeling had already passed off without proving anything to her, only irritating and exasperating her by its falsity. She was sitting by the window, feeling miserable and cross. It is only by being in trouble that people can understand how far from easy it is to be the master of one's feelings and thoughts. Sofya Petrovna said afterwards that there was a tangle within her which it was as difficult to unravel as to count a flock of sparrows rapidly flying by. From the fact that she was not overjoyed to see her husband, that she did not like his manner at dinner, she concluded all of a sudden that she was beginning to hate her husband.

Andrey Ilyitch, languid with hunger and exhaustion, fell upon the sausage while waiting for the soup to be brought in, and ate it greedily, munching noisily and moving his temples.

"My goodness!" thought Sofya Petrovna. "I love and respect him, but . . . why does he munch so repulsively?"

The disorder in her thoughts was no less than the disorder in her feelings. Like all persons inexperienced in combating unpleasant ideas, Madame Lubyantsev did her utmost not to think of her trouble, and the harder she tried the more vividly Ilyin, the sand on his knees, the fluffy clouds, the train, stood out in her imagination.

"And why did I go there this afternoon like a fool?" she thought, tormenting herself. "And am I really so weak that I cannot depend upon myself?"

Fear magnifies danger. By the time Andrey Ilyitch was finishing the last course, she had firmly made up her mind to tell her husband everything and to flee from danger!

"I've something serious to say to you, Andrey," she began after dinner while her husband was taking off his coat and boots to lie down for a nap.

"Well?"

"Let us leave this place!"

"H'm! . . . Where shall we go? It's too soon to go back to town."

"No; for a tour or something of that sort.

"For a tour . . ." repeated the notary, stretching. "I dream of that myself, but where are we to get the money, and to whom am I to leave the office?"

And thinking a little he added:

"Of course, you must be bored. Go by yourself if you like."

Sofya Petrovna agreed, but at once reflected that Ilyin would be delighted with the opportunity, and would go with her in the same train, in the same compartment. . . . She thought and looked at her husband, now satisfied but still languid. For some reason her eyes rested on his feet—miniature, almost feminine feet, clad in striped socks; there was a thread standing out at the tip of each sock.

Behind the blind a bumble-bee was beating itself against the window-pane and buzzing. Sofya Petrovna looked at the threads on the socks, listened to the bee, and pictured how she would set off . . . . vis-à-vis Ilyin would sit, day and night, never taking his eyes off her, wrathful at his own weakness and pale with spiritual agony. He would call himself an immoral schoolboy, would abuse her, tear his hair, but when darkness came on and the passengers were asleep or got out at a station, he would seize the opportunity to kneel before her and embrace her knees as he had at the seat in the wood. . . .

She caught herself indulging in this day-dream.

"Listen. I won't go alone," she said. "You must come with me."

"Nonsense, Sofotchka!" sighed Lubyantsev. "One must be sensible and not want the impossible."

"You will come when you know all about it," thought Sofya Petrovna.

Making up her mind to go at all costs, she felt that she was out of danger. Little by little her ideas grew clearer; her spirits rose and she allowed herself to think about it all, feeling that however much she thought, however much she dreamed, she would go away. While her husband was asleep, the evening gradually came on. She sat in the drawing-room and played the piano. The greater liveliness out of doors, the sound of music, but above all the thought that she was a sensible person, that she had surmounted her difficulties, completely restored her spirits. Other women, her appeased conscience told her, would probably have been carried off their feet in her position, and would have lost their balance, while she had almost died of shame, had been miserable, and was now running out of the danger which perhaps did not exist! She was so touched by her own virtue and determination that she even looked at herself two or three times in the looking-glass.

When it got dark, visitors arrived. The men sat down in the dining-room to play cards; the ladies remained in the drawing-room and the verandah. The last to arrive was Ilyin. He was gloomy, morose, and looked ill. He sat down in the corner of the sofa and did not move the whole evening. Usually good-humoured and talkative, this time he remained silent, frowned, and rubbed his eyebrows. When he had to answer some question, he gave a forced smile with his upper lip only, and answered jerkily and irritably. Four or five times he made some jest, but his jests sounded harsh and cutting. It seemed to Sofya Petrovna that he was on the verge of hysterics. Only now, sitting at the piano, she recognized fully for the first time that this unhappy man was in deadly earnest, that his soul was sick, and that he could find no rest. For her sake he was wasting the best days of his youth and his career, spending the last of his money on a summer villa, abandoning his mother and sisters, and, worst of all, wearing himself out in an agonizing struggle with himself. From mere common humanity he ought to be treated seriously.

She recognized all this clearly till it made her heart ache, and if at that moment she had gone up to him and said to him, "No," there would have been a force in her voice hard to disobey. But she did not go up to him and did not speak—indeed, never thought of doing so. The pettiness and egoism of youth had never been more patent in her than that evening. She realized that Ilyin was unhappy, and that he was sitting on the sofa as though he were on hot coals; she felt sorry for him, but at the same time the presence of a man who loved her to distraction, filled her soul with triumph and a sense of her own power. She felt her youth, her beauty, and her unassailable virtue, and, since she had decided to go away, gave herself full licence for that evening. She flirted, laughed incessantly, sang with peculiar feeling and gusto. Everything delighted and amused her. She was amused at the memory of what had happened at the seat in the wood, of the sentinel who had looked on. She was amused by her guests, by Ilyin's cutting jests, by the pin in his cravat, which she had never noticed before. There was a red snake with diamond eyes on the pin; this snake struck her as so amusing that she could have kissed it on the spot.

Sofya Petrovna sang nervously, with defiant recklessness as though half intoxicated, and she chose sad, mournful songs which dealt with wasted hopes, the past, old age, as though in mockery of another's grief. "'And old age comes nearer and nearer' . . ." she sang. And what was old age to her?

"It seems as though there is something going wrong with me," she thought from time to time through her laughter and singing.

The party broke up at twelve o'clock. Ilyin was the last to leave. Sofya Petrovna was still reckless enough to accompany him to the bottom step of the verandah. She wanted to tell him that she was going away with her husband, and to watch the effect this news would produce on him.

The moon was hidden behind the clouds, but it was light enough for Sofya Petrovna to see how the wind played with the skirts of his overcoat and with the awning of the verandah. She could see, too, how white Ilyin was, and how he twisted his upper lip in the effort to smile.

"Sonia, Sonitchka . . . my darling woman!" he muttered, preventing her from speaking. "My dear! my sweet!"

In a rush of tenderness, with tears in his voice, he showered caressing words upon her, that grew tenderer and tenderer, and even called her "thou," as though she were his wife or mistress. Quite unexpectedly he put one arm round her waist and with the other hand took hold of her elbow.

"My precious! my delight!" he whispered, kissing the nape of her neck; "be sincere; come to me at once!"

She slipped out of his arms and raised her head to give vent to her indignation and anger, but the indignation did not come off, and all her vaunted virtue and chastity was only sufficient to enable her to utter the phrase used by all ordinary women on such occasions:

"You must be mad."

"Come, let us go," Ilyin continued. "I felt just now, as well as at the seat in the wood, that you are as helpless as I am, Sonia . . . . You are in the same plight! You love me and are fruitlessly trying to appease your conscience. . . ."

Seeing that she was moving away, he caught her by her lace cuff and said rapidly:

"If not today, then tomorrow you will have to give in! Why, then, this waste of time? My precious, darling Sonia, the sentence is passed; why put off the execution? Why deceive yourself?"

Sofya Petrovna tore herself from him and darted in at the door. Returning to the drawing-room, she mechanically shut the piano, looked for a long time at the music-stand, and sat down. She could not stand up nor think. All that was left of her excitement and recklessness was a fearful weakness, apathy, and dreariness. Her conscience whispered to her that she had behaved badly, foolishly, that evening, like some madcap girl—that she had just been embraced on the verandah, and still had an uneasy feeling in her waist and her elbow. There was not a soul in the drawing-room; there was only one candle burning. Madame Lubyantsev sat on the round stool before the piano, motionless, as though expecting something. And as though taking advantage of the darkness and her extreme lassitude, an oppressive, overpowering desire began to assail her. Like a boa-constrictor it gripped her limbs and her soul, and grew stronger every second, and no longer menaced her as it had done, but stood clear before her in all its nakedness.

She sat for half an hour without stirring, not restraining herself from thinking of Ilyin, then she got up languidly and dragged herself to her bedroom. Andrey Ilyitch was already in bed. She sat down by the open window and gave herself up to desire. There was no "tangle" now in her head; all her thoughts and feelings were bent with one accord upon a single aim. She tried to struggle against it, but instantly gave it up. . . . She understood now how strong and relentless was the foe. Strength and fortitude were needed to combat him, and her birth, her education, and her life had given her nothing to fall back upon.

"Immoral wretch! Low creature!" she nagged at herself for her weakness. "So that's what you're like!"

Her outraged sense of propriety was moved to such indignation by this weakness that she lavished upon herself every term of abuse she knew, and told herself many offensive and humiliating truths. So, for instance, she told herself that she never had been moral, that she had not come to grief before simply because she had had no opportunity, that her inward conflict during that day had all been a farce. . . .

"And even if I have struggled," she thought, "what sort of struggle was it? Even the woman who sells herself struggles before she brings herself to it, and yet she sells herself. A fine struggle! Like milk, I've turned in a day! In one day!"

She convicted herself of being tempted, not by feeling, not by Ilyin personally, but by sensations which awaited her . . . an idle lady, having her fling in the summer holidays, like so many!

"'Like an unfledged bird when the mother has been slain,'" sang a husky tenor outside the window.

"If I am to go, it's time," thought Sofya Petrovna. Her heart suddenly began beating violently.

"Andrey!" she almost shrieked. "Listen! we . . . we are going? Yes?"

"Yes, I've told you already: you go alone."

"But listen," she began. "If you don't go with me, you are in danger of losing me. I believe I am . . . in love already."

"With whom?" asked Andrey Ilyitch.

"It can't make any difference to you who it is!" cried Sofya Petrovna.

Andrey Ilyitch sat up with his feet out of bed and looked wonderingly at his wife's dark figure.

"It's a fancy!" he yawned.

He did not believe her, but yet he was frightened. After thinking a little and asking his wife several unimportant questions, he delivered himself of his opinions on the family, on infidelity . . . spoke listlessly for about ten minutes and got into bed again. His moralizing produced no effect. There are a great many opinions in the world, and a good half of them are held by people who have never been in trouble!

In spite of the late hour, summer visitors were still walking outside. Sofya Petrovna put on a light cape, stood a little, thought a little. . . . She still had resolution enough to say to her sleeping husband:

"Are you asleep? I am going for a walk. . . . Will you come with me?"

That was her last hope. Receiving no answer, she went out. . . . It was fresh and windy. She was conscious neither of the wind nor the darkness, but went on and on. . . . An overmastering force drove her on, and it seemed as though, if she had stopped, it would have pushed her in the back.

"Immoral creature!" she muttered mechanically. "Low wretch!"

She was breathless, hot with shame, did not feel her legs under her, but what drove her on was stronger than shame, reason, or fear.

NOTES

making love to me: in the 19th century this meant declaring one's love, courting

vis-à-vis: face to face

Sofotchka: an affectionate diminutive form of Sofya

Sonitchka: another affectionate diminutive form of Sofya

"thou": the familiar form of "you" that is used in Russian to address family members and children

A TRIFLE FROM LIFE

A well-fed, red-cheeked young man called Nikolay Ilyitch Belyaev, of thirty-two, who was an owner of house property in Petersburg, and a devotee of the race-course, went one evening to see Olga Ivanovna Irnin, with whom he was living, or, to use his own expression, was dragging out a long, wearisome romance. And, indeed, the first interesting and enthusiastic pages of this romance had long been perused; now the pages dragged on, and still dragged on, without presenting anything new or of interest.

Not finding Olga Ivanovna at home, my hero lay down on the lounge chair and proceeded to wait for her in the drawing-room.

"Good-evening, Nikolay Ilyitch!" he heard a child's voice. "Mother will be here directly. She has gone with Sonia to the dressmaker's."

Olga Ivanovna's son, Alyosha—a boy of eight who looked graceful and very well cared for, who was dressed like a picture, in a black velvet jacket and long black stockings—was lying on the sofa in the same room. He was lying on a satin cushion and, evidently imitating an acrobat he had lately seen at the circus, stuck up in the air first one leg and then the other. When his elegant legs were exhausted, he brought his arms into play or jumped up impulsively and went on all fours, trying to stand with his legs in the air. All this he was doing with the utmost gravity, gasping and groaning painfully as though he regretted that God had given him such a restless body.

"Ah, good-evening, my boy," said Belyaev. "It's you! I did not notice you. Is your mother well?"

Alyosha, taking hold of the tip of his left toe with his right hand and falling into the most unnatural attitude, turned over, jumped up, and peeped at Belyaev from behind the big fluffy lampshade.

"What shall I say?" he said, shrugging his shoulders. "In reality mother's never well. You see, she is a woman, and women, Nikolay Ilyitch, have always something the matter with them."

Belyaev, having nothing better to do, began watching Alyosha's face. He had never before during the whole of his intimacy with Olga Ivanovna paid any attention to the boy, and had completely ignored his existence; the boy had been before his eyes, but he had not cared to think why he was there and what part he was playing.

In the twilight of the evening, Alyosha's face, with his white forehead and black, unblinking eyes, unexpectedly reminded Belyaev of Olga Ivanovna as she had been during the first pages of their romance. And he felt disposed to be friendly to the boy.

"Come here, insect," he said; "let me have a closer look at you."

The boy jumped off the sofa and skipped up to Belyaev.

"Well," began Nikolay Ilyitch, putting a hand on the boy's thin shoulder. "How are you getting on?"

"How shall I say! We used to get on a great deal better."

"Why?"

"It's very simple. Sonia and I used only to learn music and reading, and now they give us French poetry to learn. Have you been shaved lately?"

"Yes."

"Yes, I see you have. Your beard is shorter. Let me touch it. . . . Does that hurt?"

"No."

"Why is it that if you pull one hair it hurts, but if you pull a lot at once it doesn't hurt a bit? Ha, ha! And, you know, it's a pity you don't have whiskers. Here ought to be shaved . . . but here at the sides the hair ought to be left. . . ."

The boy nestled up to Belyaev and began playing with his watch-chain.

"When I go to the high-school," he said, "mother is going to buy me a watch. I shall ask her to buy me a watch-chain like this. . . . What a lo-ket! Father's got a locket like that, only yours has little bars on it and his has letters. . . . There's mother's portrait in the middle of his. Father has a different sort of chain now, not made with rings, but like ribbon. . . ."

"How do you know? Do you see your father?"

"I? M'm . . . no . . . I . . ."

Alyosha blushed, and in great confusion, feeling caught in a lie, began zealously scratching the locket with his nail. . . . Belyaev looked steadily into his face and asked:

"Do you see your father?"

"N-no!"

"Come, speak frankly, on your honour. . . . I see from your face you are telling a fib. Once you've let a thing slip out it's no good wriggling about it. Tell me, do you see him? Come, as a friend."

Alyosha hesitated.

"You won't tell mother?" he said.

"As though I should!"

"On your honour?"

"On my honour."

"Do you swear?"

"Ah, you provoking boy! What do you take me for?"

Alyosha looked round him, then with wide-open eyes, whispered to him:

"Only, for goodness' sake, don't tell mother. . . . Don't tell any one at all, for it is a secret. I hope to goodness mother won't find out, or we should all catch it—Sonia, and I, and Pelagea . . . . Well, listen. . . Sonia and I see father every Tuesday and Friday. When Pelagea takes us for a walk before dinner we go to the Apfel Restaurant, and there is father waiting for us. . . . He is always sitting in a room apart, where you know there's a marble table and an ash-tray in the shape of a goose without a back. . . ."

"What do you do there?"

"Nothing! First we say how-do-you-do, then we all sit round the table, and father treats us with coffee and pies. You know Sonia eats the meat-pies, but I can't endure meat-pies! I like the pies made of cabbage and eggs. We eat such a lot that we have to try hard to eat as much as we can at dinner, for fear mother should notice."

"What do you talk about?"

"With father? About anything. He kisses us, he hugs us, tells us all sorts of amusing jokes. Do you know, he says when we are grown up he is going to take us to live with him. Sonia does not want to go, but I agree. Of course, I should miss mother; but, then, I should write her letters! It's a queer idea, but we could come and visit her on holidays—couldn't we? Father says, too, that he will buy me a horse. He's an awfully kind man! I can't understand why mother does not ask him to come and live with us, and why she forbids us to see him. You know he loves mother very much. He is always asking us how she is and what she is doing. When she was ill he clutched his head like this, and . . . and kept running about. He always tells us to be obedient and respectful to her. Listen. Is it true that we are unfortunate?"

"H'm! . . . Why?"

"That's what father says. 'You are unhappy children,' he says. It's strange to hear him, really. 'You are unhappy,' he says, 'I am unhappy, and mother's unhappy. You must pray to God,' he says; 'for yourselves and for her.'"

Alyosha let his eyes rest on a stuffed bird and sank into thought.

"So . . ." growled Belyaev. "So that's how you are going on. You arrange meetings at restaurants. And mother does not know?"

"No-o. . . . How should she know? Pelagea would not tell her for anything, you know. The day before yesterday he gave us some pears. As sweet as jam! I ate two."

"H'm! . . . Well, and I say . . Listen. Did father say anything about me?"

"About you? What shall I say?"

Alyosha looked searchingly into Belyaev's face and shrugged his shoulders.

"He didn't say anything particular."

"For instance, what did he say?"

"You won't be offended?"

"What next? Why, does he abuse me?"

"He doesn't abuse you, but you know he is angry with you. He says mother's unhappy owing to you . . . and that you have ruined mother. You know he is so queer! I explain to him that you are kind, that you never scold mother; but he only shakes his head."

"So he says I have ruined her?"

"Yes; you mustn't be offended, Nikolay Ilyitch."

Belyaev got up, stood still a moment, and walked up and down the drawing-room.

"That's strange and . . . ridiculous!" he muttered, shrugging his shoulders and smiling sarcastically. "He's entirely to blame, and I have ruined her, eh? An innocent lamb, I must say. So he told you I ruined your mother?"

"Yes, but . . . you said you would not be offended, you know."

"I am not offended, and . . . and it's not your business. Why, it's . . . why, it's positively ridiculous! I have been thrust into it like a chicken in the broth, and now it seems I'm to blame!"

A ring was heard. The boy sprang up from his place and ran out. A minute later a lady came into the room with a little girl; this was Olga Ivanovna, Alyosha's mother. Alyosha followed them in, skipping and jumping, humming aloud and waving his hands. Belyaev nodded, and went on walking up and down.

"Of course, whose fault is it if not mine?" he muttered with a snort. "He is right! He is an injured husband."

"What are you talking about?" asked Olga Ivanovna.

"What about? . . . Why, just listen to the tales your lawful spouse is spreading now! It appears that I am a scoundrel and a villain, that I have ruined you and the children. All of you are unhappy, and I am the only happy one! Wonderfully, wonderfully happy!"

"I don't understand, Nikolay. What's the matter?"

"Why, listen to this young gentleman!" said Belyaev, pointing to Alyosha.

Alyosha flushed crimson, then turned pale, and his whole face began working with terror.

"Nikolay Ilyitch," he said in a loud whisper. "Sh-sh!"

Olga Ivanovna looked in surprise at Alyosha, then at Belyaev, then at Alyosha again.

"Just ask him," Belyaev went on. "Your Pelagea, like a regular fool, takes them about to restaurants and arranges meetings with their papa. But that's not the point: the point is that their dear papa is a victim, while I'm a wretch who has broken up both your lives. . ."

"Nikolay Ilyitch," moaned Alyosha. "Why, you promised on your word of honour!"

"Oh, get away!" said Belyaev, waving him off. "This is more important than any word of honour. It's the hypocrisy revolts me, the lying! . . ."

"I don't understand it," said Olga Ivanovna, and tears glistened in her eyes. "Tell me, Alyosha," she turned to her son. "Do you see your father?"

Alyosha did not hear her; he was looking with horror at Belyaev.

"It's impossible," said his mother; "I will go and question Pelagea."

Olga Ivanovna went out.

"I say, you promised on your word of honour!" said Alyosha, trembling all over.

Belyaev dismissed him with a wave of his hand, and went on walking up and down. He was absorbed in his grievance and was oblivious of the boy's presence, as he always had been. He, a grown-up, serious person, had no thought to spare for boys. And Alyosha sat down in the corner and told Sonia with horror how he had been deceived. He was trembling, stammering, and crying. It was the first time in his life that he had been brought into such coarse contact with lying; till then he had not known that there are in the world, besides sweet pears, pies, and expensive watches, a great many things for which the language of children has no expression.

Printed in Great Britain
by Amazon

17794810R00082